SEEKER'S HUNT

SEEKER'S WORLD, BOOK FIVE

K. A. RILEY

For Tanis.

SUMMARY

War is coming to the Otherwhere, and the Orb of Kilarin is still hidden somewhere, awaiting discovery by a Seeker.

In the meantime, Vega has returned to Fairhaven. A new threat has risen in the Otherwhere's South, and there is little time left to make the ancient prophecy come true.

Betrayal, bonds, and a battle in Fairhaven will threaten Vega's life, her love, and the family she's managed to build.

Will she be able to stop the danger before all is lost?

DRAGON FLIGHT

CALLUM and I sat astride the base of Caffall's broad neck, the wind whipping at our clothing as the Otherwhere unfurled far below us like a gigantic, multicolored quilt of bald gray stone and rolling hills.

It was our last hurrah before I was to head back to my world for the next part of my school year, and the experience should have been beautiful, intimate, wondrous. It should have felt special—a miraculous, romantic date, a much-needed escape from the heavier aspects of our lives.

But instead, my mind churned with anxious thoughts of the conversation that had taken place only a day earlier, when Solara, head Witch of the Aradia Coven and descendant of the famous Sorceress Morgan Le Fay, had told us that a figure from her past had shown himself to her in a vision.

The man, she'd said, was called Meligant, and he was the long-lost brother of the Crimson King, the ruler who'd reigned over the Otherwhere for centuries. Which meant he was related to Callum, therefore had a legitimate claim to the throne of the Otherwhere.

Like Callum, Meligant was a former dragon shifter. And like

Callum, he'd been Severed from the beast inside him so they could exist as separate, independent entities.

If he was as strong as I suspected, this man could prove a deadly adversary and a cruel enemy.

Which was reason enough to worry.

But I was also possessed by a deep, nagging feeling that Meligant wasn't only after the throne. After all, if he'd wanted it, he could have gone after it many years ago.

If he'd shown himself to Solara, there had to be a reason for it. But what that reason was, I couldn't begin to speculate.

I was no Seer. I couldn't predict the future, or guess what it held. All I could do was try to control my own fate to the best of my abilities, and hope I made choices that would benefit the Otherwhere as well as my world.

Right now, though, I felt powerless. Thoughts of the man from Solara's vision were eating away at my mind, my gut, prodding me without relief.

"Vega?" Callum said softly, holding my waist from behind as Caffall soared over the exquisite landscape far below.

"Mmm?" I asked, trying my best to pull myself out of my worries and into the present.

"You all right?"

"Fine," I fibbed. "Just thinking, which is probably a bad idea."

"Always."

I forced out a chuckle then asked where we were.

"Anara is below us. The land where I was born so long ago, and spent a few happy years, before…"

His voice trailed off. It seemed I wasn't the only one whose mind was hanging around in a dark place.

"Before…" I echoed, recalling that his family had all but imprisoned him in a dank cell when he was young in an attempt to keep his inner dragon from showing itself.

The rolling green hills below us exuded a feeling of peace and comfort, a sort of cushioned welcome mat for all who were fortunate enough to visit. During Callum's early, innocent years, it seemed, his life had been near-perfect.

What his parents had done to him since was an abuse I would never forgive.

I'd seen Anara once, on my first day in the Otherwhere. It was there that I'd first laid eyes on Merriwether, my grandfather and the Headmaster of the Academy for the Blood-Born. I would always remember the feeling of calm that had permeated my every cell as I'd stood staring out at the vast lushness of the land.

It angered me beyond words to think of the pleasant life that had been torn away from Callum at such an early age.

"Can I ask you a question?" I finally said, hesitant.

"Of course."

"Your sister..." I began, pausing as I searched for the next words.

"What about her?" he replied, a slight growl entering his tone. I knew it wasn't directed at me, but it sent goosebumps rising along my skin all the same. Callum's power—his strength, his sheer air of dominance—would never fail to leave me with a sense of awe. I'd never met anyone so intimidating.

Yet he was also the kindest, most loving person I'd ever encountered.

His sister was a sore subject, and it was no wonder. The woman known as the Usurper Queen had stolen the Otherwhere's throne from him—with the help of their awful parents. She'd all but banished him from the land.

Not to mention that she'd imprisoned my brother, my best friend, and me, locked five exquisite dragons in cruel, diminutive cages, and tortured them in hopes of bending them to her will.

She wasn't exactly Callum's favorite person, and I wasn't particularly fond of her, either.

"Would you rather I didn't ask about her?" I said.

"I'm sorry," he replied, his fingers tightening their hold on my waist. "You know you can ask me anything. I'll do my best to answer."

"It's more a question about someone else, anyhow."

"Oh? Who?"

"Meligant," I said. "Do you think your sister knows about his existence, his...Severing?"

"Probably. I heard stories when I was a child. Whispers. But Meligant disappeared a long time ago. My family assumed that he'd died, and I can't say anyone was unhappy about it. There were rumors that he'd once hoped to steal the throne from his brother, the Crimson King—and by the time my sister came into power..."

"Usurped the throne, you mean."

"Whatever we choose to call it," Callum said, "by the time it happened, there wasn't a soul in my family who thought Meligant was alive, let alone a threat. As for whether my sister knows, I'm sure she and that warlock husband of hers have talked about every possible threat to her reign. I couldn't say for sure, though. I haven't seen her in ages, and I have no desire to lay my eyes on her anytime soon, though I know the time is coming when I'll have no choice."

"The coming war, you mean," I replied softly.

"Yes," he said. "The war."

Below us, I felt Caffall tighten, the flapping of his wings accelerating as if the word had agitated him.

"Maybe, just for now, we should talk about something else," I said, stroking a hand along Caffall's scales.

"Agreed. This little adventure of ours was meant to be a nice, distracting outing before you head home to Fairhaven. Not a depressing discussion of my fair sister's many delightful attributes."

Chuckling, I narrowed my eyes and stared into the distance. "I'd be happy to talk about something else. For starters, maybe you could tell me what *that* is." I pointed toward the south, where a gigantic, gaping wound cut across the landscape, tearing into the southern edge of Anara as if some giant had taken a knife and ripped through the land itself.

"That's the Chasm," Callum said solemnly. "The place Solara mentioned—the one she saw in her vision. It's a giant canyon that splits the southern section of the Otherwhere off from the rest of this region. Beyond it lie what are called the Forsaken Lands."

"It's so strange-looking. Like it doesn't belong in the Otherwhere at all. It feels like…a mistake."

I was trying to sound only casually interested, but the truth was that something about the Chasm terrified me.

It awoke memories of the sickening feeling, when I was a child, of moments shrouded in darkness when I was too frightened to set my foot on the floor next to my bed for fear that monsters lurked below, waiting to reach out and pull me under.

But I was no child. Not anymore. I was meant to help heal this world, which meant taking chances and putting on a brave face, despite my fears.

"Is it safe to take a closer look?" I asked, trying my best to sound courageous.

"Let's find out. Caffall?" Callum asked, seeking his dragon's opinion. "What do you think?"

~I see no reason not to approach from above, the dragon's voice rumbled through the air, not so much a sound as a sensation of words vibrating through flesh and bone. *Unless the Chasm finds a way to suck us in, I can't fathom why we should be afraid of it.*

Still, I could feel Callum tensing once again behind me, his grip tightening protectively.

"What is it?" I asked.

"Nothing. Just a feeling…"

"We'll be all right," I replied, feigning another bout of confidence. "Caffall said we were safe to approach, and it's only right to take his word for it. He can see farther, smell more, hear more than either of us. He's our protector. I trust him."

~*Thank you, Seeker.*

"You're welcome," I said, stroking my fingers over the base of the dragon's golden neck. "I just hope you're right."

~*As do I. Come, let's take a look. I promise to remain on high alert.*

Good, I thought.

Still, I couldn't keep my breath from catching in my throat as we flew over the monstrous laceration in the landscape.

STRANGER

THE CHASM'S depths were dark and forbidding, and I was sure that at its deepest point—it must have been five hundred feet down, at least—I could see a sea of fiery red lava churning angrily, like the earth was threatening to explode at any moment.

"I'm beginning to understand why everything beyond the Chasm is dead," I said, pulling my chin up to avoid looking at the hellish sight.

The contrast between the land beyond the Chasm and the lush green of Anara was staggering. The sky beyond was the color of ash—a sickly gray, sapped of any healthy living thing.

The air twisted and spun with moving clouds of soot and ash, a toxic mess of death and destruction.

"The Forsaken Lands," Callum told me, "are nothingness. Death. If Meligant and his dragon have been surviving all these years in the South, I can't imagine how. There is nothing green. No healthy living creature. I shudder to think what he must consume—if indeed he's alive, which seems all but impossible. Still..."

Dread filled me with his utterance of the last word. "Are you saying you think there's a chance Solara's vision was real?"

Callum seemed to contemplate my question for a moment before saying, "She's a Witch, and a powerful one. She wouldn't have told us about it unless she was quite sure it *was* real. I don't know her well, but something about her feels incapable of issuing lies."

"You really think that man—Meligant—could be alive, then."

"Logic tells me it's impossible. But I *feel* that he is. Caffall does, too. There is something in the air here—something threatening that I can't quite find the words to describe. A sort of rage, twisting through the very particles around us. I wonder if that's what's fed him all these years."

"I feel it, too. It's like the air is…bitter," I said with a shudder. "We should turn back. I should never have suggested we come here."

~*If I remain unseen, there is little risk,* Caffall replied, his voice thundering in its mysterious way through the air between Callum and myself. *If indeed there is no life here, we have nothing to worry about.*

"That's a pretty big if," I replied.

~*I am watching for threats, Seeker. I will not let any harm come to either of you.*

When I'd reluctantly agreed to proceed, Caffall flew us over a knotted tangle of deep scars in the earth only to come to a series of jagged, unforgiving peaks. Here and there on the ground below, I could see the silhouette of a decaying tree outlined in dull, hazy shadow against the ash-coated ground.

Caffall was fast, and I was grateful for his unfaltering speed as a growing feeling of unease simmered inside me.

"I don't see how Solara's vision *could* be true," I said after a time, attempting to reassure myself more than anyone else. "There's no way anything lives here, not even the corrupt brother of a dead king. I don't even see a stream or river. Without water, nothing can survive long, no matter how strong it might be."

Callum replied with a deep-voiced, "Let's hope you're right."

But he was holding onto me ever more protectively, as if he could sense the same looming, invisible threat that I did.

We'd just circled a large, barren valley and were about to turn north again when a shrill cry erupted from somewhere in the distance. The dismal fog of cloud and ash obscured our view of anything more than a few hundred feet away, and I tensed, grabbing tighter to Caffall's jagged golden mane.

"What the hell was that?" I half-cried.

"Not sure," Callum replied, "but we need to get out of here and back over the Chasm to Anara. Without eyes, we're virtually defenseless in this place."

Seeming to agree, Caffall banked sharply to the right. Callum and I leaned forward, holding on hard as a winged shadow emerged from a grim twister of swirling cloud in the distance.

~*Our question,* Caffall's voice bellowed, *is answered. The silver dragon lives.*

I squinted, at first just barely able to make out the enormous flying creature coming at us. But as he approached, I could see that he was metallic, tarnished silver, a crown of pointed scales on his head like the one that had recently formed on Caffall's own.

Only the silver dragon's was more threatening and far more monstrous.

Half the crown's glimmering peaks were broken off, leaving jagged stalagmites of silver scale that looked more like deadly weapons than symbols of royalty.

His scales were patchy in places, as if he suffered from a sort of reptilian mange. No doubt it was a symptom of life in such toxic lands.

"I think the dragon might be blind," Callum said, sounding as shocked as I felt.

Examining the creature, I saw what he meant. Unlike Caffall, the silver dragon's eyes, including their pupils, were pure white and unreadable.

A man sat on the dragon's back, his spine straight, his face pale. He was dressed entirely in what may once have been elegant clothing, but now looked like decaying rags.

If I hadn't known better, I would have described him as a vaguely sentient corpse.

The two of them, decrepit-looking though they were, flew at us like a missile, narrowly missing us in mid-air as the silver dragon let out another blood-curdling shriek and banked hard to his left.

"Meligant," I mouthed involuntarily, twisting to stare back at the dragon's rider.

The man turned then and looked directly at me, his features eerily devoid of life.

"Seeker," a voice hissed through my mind. I tried to pull my eyes away, but found myself trapped in his gaze, drawn in desperately, like a crazed moth to a flame.

Why have you shown yourself, after all these years? I asked silently. *Why now?*

It was then that Meligant uttered eight words that would irreparably alter my life.

"Because the time has come to find him."

THE CHILD

CAFFALL TWISTED through the air to aim his sleek form northward, dodging a barrage of gruesome, jagged missiles of blood-red flame hurled at us from the silver dragon's throat.

A few minutes later, after what felt like an eternity of panic, we had deftly crossed the Chasm to safety, and for the first time, I found myself able to force a breath from my lungs.

Frozen into a state of near-shock, I said nothing to Callum about the strange look in the man's eye when he and I had locked gazes, or about the words that had penetrated my mind.

The time has come to find him.

Who could Meligant mean? Who, exactly, was *him*?

It wasn't until we finally landed at the Academy that I felt like I could breathe properly. When we'd dismounted, Callum and I examined Caffall to ensure that he wasn't hurt.

As I ran a hand over the dragon's neck, his voice rumbled its way into my mind, a rough, echoing whisper:

~Be wary, Vega Sloane.

Wary? I asked silently. *Of Meligant, you mean?*

But the dragon said nothing more.

Puzzled, I looked over at Callum, who was carefully perusing the thick layer of skin along Caffall's wings.

"Well, I guess we can now state with certainty that Meligant is alive," he said when he'd determined the dragon was free of wounds.

"I guess so," I replied, trying my best to sound cheerful rather than terrified.

"And you, old friend," Callum told Caffall with a final pat on the neck, "are good to go. Be careful up there. Stay away from the southern reaches for now, would you?"

~Of course, Caffall's voice vibrated through the air.

As I watched him, I was certain his extraordinary eyes locked on my own for a moment before he took off for the sky with a low, thunderous growl.

Callum took my hand when the dragon had disappeared into a bank of gray-white fluff.

"You're worried," he observed.

"A little, yeah. That was crazy." I eyed him curiously. "You don't seem quite so concerned, though…"

"Meligant may live and breathe," he said, "but if he's truly chosen to dwell beyond the Chasm…well, he can't be entirely right in the head, to put it politely. I don't think we need to concern ourselves with him."

"You don't think he's just been hiding from the world? Waiting for a chance to make his move?" I asked, trying not to give away the full depth of my concern. There was no reason our last night together had to be fraught with worry. We'd been through so much, Callum and I. There was no need to layer another serving of anxiety on top of everything we'd already suffered.

Besides, if Meligant's mind really was as far gone as Callum thought, the words I'd heard could mean anything. Or nothing, even. The rantings of a madman were hardly worth the stress I was feeling.

"Hiding? Maybe," Callum replied. "Yes. He's certainly been hiding. But why? If he wanted the throne, why not simply…take it? He has a dragon at his disposal, and he may well have allies. He could have attacked the queen—my sister—ages ago. Why wait? What's happened, that he's just now decided to come out of hiding?"

"I don't know," I said, guilt curdling my insides for keeping Meligant's words to myself. I wasn't sure why I was so reluctant to tell Callum about them.

Maybe it was fear that he would think I'd lost my mind.

After chewing on my nails for a moment, I finally mustered the courage to speak again. "Did you…happen to hear him say something when we were up there?" I asked, nodding toward the sky.

"Nothing," Callum replied. "I'm not even sure he's capable of speaking, truth be told. Why?"

I shook my head, curls flying loosely about my face, and smiled as I struggled to convince myself I'd imagined the whole thing. "No reason," I said.

"Let's head inside," Callum suggested with a brief smile. "I thought we could have a nice dinner on our last official night together—though I don't want you to forget you can come see me anytime you like. Day or night." With that, he pulled me close and kissed me, benevolently robbing me of any stray worries.

"I will come see you," I promised. "As often as I can—within reason, I mean. I *do* still need to sleep. And study. And, you know, be vaguely present in my world, if only for the sake of appearances."

"And I'll need to spend my time strategizing, gathering troops and training them. Even if Meligant turns out to be harmless, there's still a battle coming with my dear sister. I need to prepare myself as well as the Academy's fighters."

"Of course."

Relishing the strength in his voice, I pushed myself onto my toes and kissed him before adding, "There's just one thing I need to do before dinner. I'll find you in a few minutes in the Rose Wing?"

Callum cocked his head, a mischievous grin ticking the corners of his lips upward, then gave me a final kiss. "Fine. But don't be long. I've spent enough time unconscious recently that I feel I've wasted a great number of hours I could have spent with you."

"We have all sorts of time to spend together in the future," I insisted. With a gentle push and a chuckle, I added, "Go! I promise, I'll be in to see you very soon."

Callum lowered his chin playfully and raised an eyebrow. "Why do I think you're about to disappear like a magician practicing her tricks?"

"Because you know me well?"

"Mischievous girl."

"Clever boy."

After I'd watched him leave, I glanced around to make sure I was alone before summoning a Breach to Merriwether's office.

My grandfather was sitting at his desk when I arrived, and as usual, he looked as though he was anticipating my visit.

"How do you always know?" I asked.

He rose to his feet, and I could see that he was dressed in a suit of black with a purple waistcoat, white shirt, and silver tie. As always, he seemed immensely tall. Merriwether was a daunting presence—impenetrable, imposing—yet somehow he managed to exude all the warmth of a roaring hearth on a frigid winter day.

"Magic is a powerful force," he said. "For you to summon a Breach creates a certain energy that I can feel in my mind, my blood. It's why we spell-casters must occasionally resist the desire to use our skills—it's all too easy to feel our presence on the air." The corners of his eyes creased into a series of amused wrinkles. "Not to mention the full-sized door that just appeared in the middle of my office."

I turned to look at the Breach, laughing as it faded from sight. "I forgot you could see it," I said with a chuckle. "I feel like a bit of an idiot now."

"You shouldn't. You should always ask questions, Vega my dear. It's the only way to learn. Now, what can I do for you?"

"I'm wondering if Solara is still here, at the Academy. I need to speak to her."

Merriwether shook his head. "She's gone back to the Aradia Coven, I'm afraid. Left some hours ago. She'll be there already, of course, what with her particular gift for high-speed travel."

"Right—*Moving on the Wind*, she called it," I said. "I need to talk to her. I have questions."

"Yes, of course you do. The time has come for many questions to be answered. A storm is approaching, and we must all do what we need to prepare."

"A storm," I said absently. "Yes. That's exactly what it felt like."

For a second, I contemplated telling him what I'd heard Meligant say, and asking if he knew what it meant.

But my mind steered me toward Solara. Something told me she was the one I needed to ask first. She was the one who knew Meligant, after all.

"Vega," Merriwether said.

"Yes?"

"Be careful what you wish for."

"Wish for? What do you mean?"

He seated himself, took a deep breath, and said, "There is an old story of a young woman who lived in Anara many years ago. For her twentieth birthday, she was given a gift—a beautiful wooden box, with pearl inlay and exquisite carvings on the outside. She loved it for its beauty, but the woman who gave it to her—some said she was a Witch—told her never to open it. That if she did, it would bring her nothing but sorrow."

"This sounds like a fairy tale from our world," I said. "Why are they always stories of young women who are told not to do things, then do them anyhow and ruin everything? They always end up in comas, or imprisoned, while they wait for handsome men to come and plant their lips on them."

Merriwether chuckled. "Women have historically been the scapegoats for all the world's ills," he said bitterly. "And men have historically controlled much of the world's narrative. It suits them to depict women as weak."

"So, are you telling me the box contained all the world's ills?" I asked, pretending to gag.

"Not exactly. The young woman cracked it open one day to find a weapon of silver and gold—a dagger. She couldn't resist picking it up, but once she did, she found that she couldn't drop it again."

"It was stuck to her hand?"

"Worse. It became a part of her, as much as her heart or her mind. Its hilt grew into thin, tendril-like roots that melded with her flesh, piercing her very nerves, her veins. From that day on, every time she wanted to embrace someone, she risked hurting them. And every time she went to sleep, she risked hurting *herself*. Still, she grew to enjoy the feeling of the blade in her hand. A blacksmith offered to cut it away, to free her from her curse, but she declined."

"Why?"

Merriwether shrugged. "I suppose she'd become attached to it," he said with a wink.

"Clever."

"Finally one day, a suitor came to her, asking—ironically, I suppose—for her hand in marriage. Delighted, she said yes. He was a good man from a good family, and she grew quickly to love him. But before they could be wed...she killed him."

"By accident, I assume?" I said. "I mean, one hug and he'd be toast, right?"

"Perhaps it *was* an accident," Merriwether replied. "Or, more likely, she'd grown addicted to the feeling of power that came with such a weapon. It had become an obsession, a very part of her. To let go of that power would feel, quite literally, like losing a limb. And maybe she didn't wish to do that—even if it meant a chance at a quiet, happy life."

"Ah, so this is really a retelling of the myth of Pandora's Box, but with stabbing. So, the moral is…?"

"Some boxes are best left sealed. Your intentions may be innocent and pure…but when you open the box and find yourself wielding a dangerous blade, be prepared to cut someone close to you."

"Well, the good news is that I don't wield blades," I said. "At least, not often. And when I do, I usually have no idea what to do with them."

"And your incompetence with traditional weaponry is supposed to reassure me how, Granddaughter?"

"Good point," I laughed. "Don't worry. If I see a strange wooden box, I promise I'll leave it closed."

"Excellent," Merriwether said with a smile. "Now, go. Summon a Breach to Solara's home. I hope you find what you're looking for."

"I do too," I said, turning toward the far wall, closing my eyes, and calling on my power.

The faded wooden door that popped up in front of me was carved tidily with a scene of crooked houses lining a pretty street, a crescent moon hanging over the rooftops.

Smiling, I pulled the dragon key from around my neck, unlocked the door, and pushed it open, stepping through into a town several days' ride from the Academy.

ARADIA

I STEPPED out onto the street in front of a white house with green trim, a home both welcoming and daunting. The two-story structure, charming as it was, both exuded a formidable power and drew me in, like an attractive, predatory animal looking to trap its prey.

As I fixed my eyes on the front door, it flew open, beckoning me inside. I laughed, recalling the time the house's owner had told me it only ever opened for her.

"Come in, Vega," a melodious voice called out from inside.

As I stepped over the threshold, I was greeted by the bright, cheerful interior, the pristine white furnishings telling me to make myself comfortable.

Solara stepped out of the kitchen, dressed as always in head-to-toe form-fitting black clothing, a strange smile on her lips as she narrowed her exquisitely intimidating eyes at me.

"What a pleasant surprise," she said. "I wasn't expecting you—which, I must say, are four words I rarely utter."

"Hello, Solara."

Her smile faded as quickly as it had appeared.

"You've seen him," she said, her voice suddenly parched. "You've looked into Meligant's eyes."

"I have," I replied with a solemn nod.

"Tell me everything."

"Callum and I were riding Caffall at the time, over the Chasm in the south. The silver dragon attacked us…but I don't think he intended to hurt us. He could have killed us if he'd wanted to—he caught us totally off guard. But it was more like he was herding us away from the Chasm…sending us back to the Academy. I want to understand why."

"He has his reasons, no doubt," Solara said. "He wanted you to see him…but he wanted you alive, too. Which means he thinks you will serve some purpose that benefits him."

She looked me up and down, appraising, as though searching for a clue.

"You didn't only come here to ask me about his motives for leaving you unharmed. Something else prompted you to come. What is it?"

I chewed on my lip for a moment, choosing my words carefully. "I think he said something to me…I…I felt him. Inside my mind. I'm not sure if I imagined it or not, but it felt real at the time."

"If it felt real to you, Vega, then it was most likely real."

"I didn't understand what it meant, but it disturbed me so much. I don't know what to make of it, honestly."

"Come, let me get you some tea and we can discuss it." Solara must have seen me hesitating, because she added, "Don't worry. You'll be back by Callum's side soon, I promise."

"You read my mind."

"It's not difficult to surmise that your primary desire is to be with him," she said with a sly grin. "Come. Sit."

I seated myself at her kitchen table, which was white, prettily carved wood, with red-and-white striped chairs. Solara poured me a cup of tea that was reddish in color and smelled of an appealing array of spices, and sat down opposite me. The sunshine was pouring in through the broad window, warming my left side in a way that soothed and relaxed me, as if the weather itself was casting a calming spell.

"Here you go," she said, handing me my tea, which tasted like a combination of cinnamon, nutmeg, and the best, richest chocolate cake imaginable.

"Now," she said, "tell me. What exactly did Meligant say to you?"

I set my cup down and stared at it for a second before murmuring, "It'll sound so weird..."

"Nothing sounds weird to me. Trust me on that."

"I asked him why he'd come out of hiding after so many years. He said, 'Because the time has come to find him.'"

"I see," she replied, her voice quiet, pensive.

At first, she didn't say anything more.

"It seems the words came to me alone," I said. "Callum didn't hear anything. It's possible I just imagined it."

"You didn't imagine it."

"Well, I don't know why he would say a thing like that to me, of all people. I don't know Meligant, and he doesn't know me. Who is this *him* he's talking about?"

Solara looked out the window, her high cheekbones enhanced by the sunlight. "Are you certain that you want to know, Vega? Because once I tell you..."

Want? Maybe not.

But I *needed* to know.

"I am."

She let out a sigh and locked her eyes on mine. "The *him* you're wondering about...is Meligant's son. A child with whom I was once intimately connected."

"What?" I shot out, grateful that I hadn't taken another sip of tea, which would no doubt have resulted in a horrific spit-take. I stared at her a long moment before summoning the courage to ask, "Meligant's son…is he yours?"

Solara's jaw tightened, and she shook her head. "No," she said. "There was a time when Meligant wanted me to marry him. But I did not wish to leave the Coven, let alone attach myself to a man who was intent on eventually stealing his brother's throne. He was thirsty for power, and I was not."

"I see. So the mother…"

"Was the woman who married Meligant decades ago, after he and I parted ways. She died in childbirth."

"Who was she?"

Solara took a sip of tea and looked away. I'd never seen her so evasive, so reluctant to meet my gaze.

"She was my sister," she said finally.

Oh my God.

I measured my next words carefully, but there was no way to ask the question delicately. "Do you mean Sister, like another Witch in the Coven? Or your biological sister?"

"Both, actually," she replied, rising to her feet. She began to pace the kitchen slowly as the story unfolded. "My sister was a Witch, like me. She knew of my trysts with Meligant, of our…affair. Relationships with outsiders are frowned upon here, as you know. But they are tolerated, so long as we don't marry. Commitment to someone outside the Coven is met with automatic expulsion."

"But you said your sister *did* marry him?"

"She did, eventually. When I was with him, she admired him from a distance, though I never knew just how much. When I rejected his proposal at last, he moved on to her. He took advantage of her affection."

"That seems…" I began.

"Cruel?" Solara asked with a snicker. "I suppose I wouldn't have minded so much, were it not for the fact that he was only using her."

"To make you jealous?"

"Jealousy is for the weak," she sneered. "I wasn't jealous. I was *angry*. He was robbing the Aradia Coven of one of our most powerful Witches—another descendant of the great Morgan Le Fay—all because he believed that the melding of his blood and hers would result in offspring so powerful that no force, no army would be able to defeat them. Think of it—a dragon shifter and a Witch of the highest order. It was a genetic dream, at least to a man like Meligant."

"I suppose that *would* be impressive," I said. "But I still don't understand...what happened?"

Solara stopped pacing and stared at me. "As I said, Meligant took my sister from me. From my Coven. He brought her to his home—a modest castle on the east coast, some way south of the Academy—and married her in a secret ceremony. Within weeks, she was carrying his child—a boy, the Seers said. Naturally, Meligant was pleased. He spoke of nothing but the power this child would carry with him. His potential to overthrow any monarch, to rule the Otherwhere with fire, magic, and fury."

"Sounds like a great dad," I said, sarcasm practically dripping from my lips.

"My sister—Tarrah was her name—realized too late that she was nothing more than a pawn to him. An incubator for his weaponized offspring. She came to me when she was six months pregnant and asked me to help her."

"What did you do?"

Solara finally sat back down, her long, elegant fingers knitting together on the table in front of her.

"I told her she needed to hide until the child was born, and never to let Meligant near him. We couldn't keep her at the Coven—he'd have found his way to her before long. And she was growing so very weak. The pregnancy was brutally hard on her mind and body—perhaps because of her expulsion from the Coven."

"Expulsion means losing your powers?" I asked.

"To some extent, yes. Tarrah had always been a gifted healer, among other things. But when she left, she lost her ability to cast spells. She became more human. Weaker. But Meligant didn't care. He knew her expulsion wouldn't affect their child's potential. He wanted the blood of Morgan Le Fay to flow through his son's veins."

Solara pressed her hands to the table, tensing for a moment before relaxing again.

"For all the healing powers of our Sisters in the Coven, we found ourselves unable to help her. So I brought her to a place far from here, to a Witch called Suspiria, who offered to conceal her for as long as she needed."

I bit my lip, terrified to hear the tale's conclusion. "What happened then?" I said, my voice tremulous.

"As I told you," she said quietly, "she died giving birth to *his* child—the child he wanted to raise to lead armies of mortals to their deaths. I went to Tarrah in the final days, devastated to know I would lose her…that I was powerless to help. She asked me to look after her son. To keep him from his father. So I did the only thing I could think of—the only thing that would be sure to send him beyond Meligant's reach."

I stared at Solara, assessing. Surely she wasn't saying…

"No," she said, shaking her head. "I didn't kill him, Vega. You know me better than that."

"I never said—"

"No. But you were thinking it." She sighed. "Not that I can blame you. The thought did cross my mind, if only for a fleeting, horrible moment. Meligant had grown angrier, crueler, since he'd learned he was to be a father. From a distance, I saw in him a sort of growing malice—a deep, dark desire to control another being, to take possession of his mind. All I wanted was to get my nephew, an innocent, beautiful infant, as far away from him as possible."

"Something tells me that didn't go over well with Meligant."

"A message was sent to him that the boy had died alongside his mother, and Meligant had little choice but to believe it."

"What happened to the child?"

"I asked Suspiria—the Witch who'd helped my sister—to take the boy away. To hide him from everyone, even me, and see to it that he was raised in a place where he wouldn't be influenced by his father's cruel ambitions or even by our Coven. I wanted him to remain ignorant of who he was." Solara clenched her hands into fists then released them again, like she was struggling against some inner demon. "It was the most difficult thing I've ever done. Saying goodbye to my sister's child—sending him from me without ever getting to know him—I was losing the only remaining part of my family."

"So you don't know where Suspiria went with the child?"

Solara frowned. "I asked her never to tell me. If I was to let him go, I needed to sever all bonds with him. That meant trying my best to rid my mind of him." She let out a heavy breath. "I conjured a spell to forget his face, his scent, his eyes, even. I never wanted to recognize him, even if I were to run into him by chance. That...was seventy years ago."

"Seventy years. Wow." I went silent for a long moment, hesitating before adding, "Your nephew must be..."

"Old?" she said. "Perhaps. But perhaps not."

When I shot Solara a perplexed look, she let out a quiet laugh. "I told you, it's complicated."

"Because Meligant ages slowly, you mean. So his child would, too?"

"That's not *quite* what I mean," she said with a quiet, sad chuckle. "You see, when I gave the baby to Suspiria, she promised she'd open a Temporal Portal before taking him to his final destination."

"Temporal Portal?" I echoed.

"Suspiria had a rare gift. She was capable of leaping not only between worlds, but through time. Just as you move through the doors you conjure, she was able to move through years—centuries, even—and back again."

"Wait—actual *time travel*? I thought that was…"

"Impossible? No. Not for her. Suspiria was able to create a sort of tunnel that cut through years like a knife through butter. She could bring herself to any era she chose. I asked her to take him somewhere safe. Somewhere far enough that I could forget he existed, at least for a little. I didn't want to wonder each time I saw a young man if he was the one I'd given away. Didn't want to think about him, not if I could help it—because if I did, I'd just want to find him and take him in. So Suspiria took him away—whether to the past or the future, I don't know. I've never seen her since."

"That's…a lot," I said, sitting back and tucking a strand of hair behind my ear. "So he could be anywhere? He could still be a baby. Or maybe he'll be a baby fifty years from now, or a hundred. Maybe he doesn't even exist in our time."

"Maybe." She let out a cynical snicker. "You must think me a horrible person, abandoning my nephew that way instead of fighting for him. I want you to know that what I did, I did for him and for my sister. The one thing I dreaded more than losing my own life was losing my flesh and blood to Meligant's greed. I wanted the child to have a chance at a quiet, peaceful life. A good life. I wanted him to know calm and goodness, rather than cruelty and avarice."

"Is there a chance your nephew is out there, like Meligant seems to think?" I asked. "Do you think there's a chance you'd know him if you saw him now?"

She shook her head. "Even if I walked straight into him, I wouldn't know him. The spell I cast when I said goodbye was meant to rid me of any bond between us. It's entirely possible that I've come close to him over the years—that our paths have crossed in this town or that. That is the curse I inflicted upon myself, both for his protection and my own."

"Well, for the record, I don't think you're horrible," I said. "You wanted your sister's child to have a shot at a life without a tyrant for a father. You didn't want him to have to suffer. You did what your sister would have wanted, and you should be proud."

"Some people wouldn't see it that way, and I can't say I blame them for it. But I like to think Tarrah's son is out there somewhere in the universe—whatever century he may live in—and that he's happy. I *need* to think that, because the alternative..." She went silent for a moment, her eyes distant. "The alternative is pain—for more people than just my sister's child."

"What are you saying?"

"The fact that Meligant is searching for the boy—that he's on the hunt—means that Tarrah's son is in danger. Which means I may need to find him—I may need to break down the wall I put up so long ago. It means letting myself feel again."

"Would that be so bad?" I asked.

"The very thought of it," she replied, "terrifies me to my very core."

LAST NIGHT

"I'm sorry," I said, staring into Solara's eyes. "I can't imagine how that must feel. To have to part with your only family member like that, and yet know he's out there somewhere…it's heartbreaking."

"You've experienced more loss in your young life than anyone should. I suspect you can indeed imagine it, Vega."

My shoulders slumped and I swallowed hard, trying to maintain my composure.

She was right.

I was all too familiar with loss and grief.

"One thing is for sure," Solara added. "If Meligant finds his son, and if he's alive, he will try to twist him into something cruel. To cultivate his ambition, to foster a desire for power. He will try to extract from his son all the gifts bestowed upon him by both the two impressive bloodlines of his parents."

"You said *if he's alive*. Is there a way to find out? Can one of the Witches from your Coven…*see* him?"

Solara shook her head. "No. Not without a Seer's stone powerful enough to break through the shrouding spell I cast so long ago. There's no telling where he might be, who he might be with." Huffing out a breath, she bowed her head. "I suppose it's for the best. If he's alive, he would do well to remain anonymous."

I took another sip of tea, my mind reeling. "Don't you think a son of Meligant's would have figured out by now that he's… special? I mean, he *must* have powers. He must be strong, at least. There's no way he's a regular human. What if he's a dragon shifter, like—" I said, cutting myself off when I saw Solara's expression sour.

Meligant was a touchy subject, at best.

"Like his father?" Solara winced slightly as she uttered the last word. "If he is a dragon shifter, then he won't be able to keep the dragon quiet forever. No dragon shifter can. But it is my hope that he inherited some combination of his parents' traits. He wouldn't necessarily have a dragon dwelling inside him as, say, Callum did for a century. He's likely filled with magic, as well as mayhem. A Witch possesses quiet powers, just as a wizard does— sometimes the power to control nature itself. But even if Tarrah's son is alive, it's very possible that he has no idea what he truly is. Just as you may never have known you were a Seeker, had Callum not stepped into your life on your seventeenth birthday."

"How do you know about that?" I retorted, but quickly chastised myself for asking such a question. "Never mind. You just do."

A thin smile worked its way over Solara's lips. "I just do."

Finally, she pushed her chair back, rose to her feet, and waved a hand through the air above the table. The tea cups, the teapot, and everything else disappeared, and the next thing I knew, we were standing outside her house.

Another impressive aspect of her magic I'd never seen.

"You want to know how I did that," she said, reading my mind.

"I'm curious, I'll admit."

"I seem to recall a joke in your world. *How do you get to Carnegie Hall?*"

I shrugged. "How?"

"Practice, practice, practice. Now, go back to your Callum. Enjoy yourself. And promise me you won't become consumed with Meligant's own obsession. You have more important things to focus on than a long-lost child who should probably stay lost."

I was about to summon a Breach when Solara added, "There's just one thing."

"What is it?"

"If you should ever discover where the boy is..."

"Yes?"

"Please tell me. Even if you think it will hurt me. If he is found, I want—*need*—to know. He will be in great danger if Meligant finds his way to him."

With a nod, I left her, stunned that the most powerful woman I'd ever met was powerless to find her own sister's child.

And hoping, if only for her sake, that I would somehow discover his whereabouts before Meligant did.

WHEN I GOT BACK to the Academy, I found Callum waiting for me at the entrance to the Rose Wing, the secluded section of the sprawling building that Merriwether had given us for our private quarters. Highlighted by white walls covered in eternally blooming red roses, beautifully veined marble, and luxurious light flooding in through its windows, the wing was fit for royalty.

I felt entirely undeserving of such a residence.

Until I simply reminded myself that I was sharing it with the heir to the throne of the Otherwhere.

As Callum and I headed down the hall toward our suite, I began to wonder if this was what it felt like to live in a monarch's palace. What must it be like to rule over a land such as the Otherwhere, and to know nothing but luxury for the rest of one's life?

Then again, monarchs didn't exactly sit around and eat bonbons all day. It seemed, in fact, that their lives consisted mostly of worrying about uprisings, potential usurpers, war, or general societal chaos.

In many ways, being a ruler sounded like the most difficult and least rewarding job in the world.

"So, Little Miss Silent," Callum said, taking my hand as we approached the massive, almost invisible doors that opened into our suite, "what's on your mind?"

He hadn't asked where I'd been, or who I'd seen during the minutes we'd spent apart. But I could tell he was curious.

And I didn't like keeping secrets from him.

"I went to see my grandfather. Then Solara," I confessed.

"Solara? Should I even ask why?"

"There's something I think you should know. Something that happened after we flew over the Chasm…though I doubted my mind at first."

"Ah. Well then, let's have a talk."

When we'd settled into the suite, Callum poured each of us a glass of ice water and we sat down on the comfortable, oversized couch. I toyed with my glass for a moment before telling him about Meligant's words, Solara's revelation about her sister's child, and the Witch Suspiria.

"So," Callum said, "it seems Meligant is more rational than I gave him credit for."

I nodded sullenly. "For whatever reason, he wants to find his child after all this time," I said. "I suspect it has to do with the fight for the throne. What confuses me is why now? Why has Meligant shown himself to Solara, to us? What's changed?"

"Maybe it's the first time he's sensed his son's presence," Callum asked with a pensive glance out the window toward the sea.

"What do you mean?"

"You said the Witch who took the boy traveled in time. For all we know, she brought him to this very year."

"But that would mean he'd still be a baby. I can't imagine Meligant would want to take care of an infant. From the looks of the Southern Lands, a baby wouldn't survive there for more than a day."

"True," Callum replied with a scratch of his chin. "Well, like you say, there has to be a reason for this timing."

He fell silent for a minute before adding, "Look—I know this is important. But the man we saw riding that dragon—he wasn't all there. He seemed all but dead inside. Maybe it's best that we leave Meligant and his rambling fantasies alone. This is our last night together before you go back to Fairhaven, so I'd rather not spend it wondering about a child who may or may not exist. I don't want to talk about the throne, my sister, my mad great-uncle, or anything…except for you and me. You and I have fought long and hard, and frankly, you must be exhausted. I know I am."

My first instinct was to protest. To insist that we talk further about the child who may or may not have grown into a man by now—particularly if he posed a threat.

But Callum was right. Speculating would only drive us both insane.

My lips twitched into a smile as he took hold of one of my dark ringlets with his fingertips. He leaned forward and kissed me gently, pressing his forehead to mine. "My Vega," he said. "Do you ever wonder what the future really looks like? I mean, aside from the myriad complications that seem to arise every time we turn around?"

"Sometimes," I replied with a chuckle. "But all that really matters to me is knowing you're in it somewhere."

"Good. Because I fully intend to be."

"In the meantime," I sighed, "I have to finish high school. It's crazy to think I'll be going back there in a day or two, like it's a normal Monday and nothing out of the ordinary has happened. No one will even so much as notice Lachlan and I were gone, yet we've been here for *weeks*." A grim memory flooded my mind then. "I'm not even the same person I was when I walked through the last door into the Otherwhere. So much has happened...so much has changed. For days, I thought you were going to die, Callum."

"But I didn't, thanks largely to you." His lips brushed mine again. "And for what it's worth, you *are* the same person. But even more beautiful, if that's possible."

"Thank you, but you forgot to add a little more *damaged*," I laughed. "As, I'm sure, is Lachlan, after everything we've been through."

I hadn't given Lachlan much thought in the past day or so—he was staying in another wing of the Academy with my fellow Seekers, Oleana, Meg, and Desmond, who were patiently awaiting our departure the following morning.

"Lachlan is fortunate to have you," Callum said. "You're a good friend to him. I hope he appreciates you as much as he should."

I shook my head, dark curls flying around my face. "I'm the one who's fortunate," I protested. "He's got some serious scars from wounds he took defending me. I'm just glad he's got a wolf inside him, or I might be dead."

"I'm grateful to him. And his wolf."

Callum threw me an odd look that prompted me to ask what he was thinking.

"I'm suddenly finding it strange to talk about people capable of shape-shifting when I've lost that power. Though..."

"Though?"

His eyes were twinkling—or was it simply the waning daylight?

"What is it?" I asked. "What's going on?"

"While you were out seeing Solara, I went to the Grove to think a little and test a theory."

"Okay..."

"I no longer have a dragon inside me. But ever since Caffall and I were Severed, I've had these...I don't know....moments of clarity."

"Moments of clarity? You mean, like visions?"

I braced myself for the worst. It was enough to have heard about Solara's visions of Meligant. I didn't want any more bad or weird news.

"Thoughts of fire and flame," Callum replied. "But not in a destructive way. It's never that the world is burning, or anything like that. More like...my mind is learning to control them, to harness fire as a dragon would. It's as if I'm inside Caffall's mind, and he in mine. Like I can feel what it is to be a dragon once again—even though I'll always exist in human flesh."

There were students at the Academy called Sparkers—fighters who could harness the power of flame and fling fireballs at their enemies.

But I had the distinct feeling Callum was talking about something else.

I pulled back and shot him a skeptical look. "Callum Drake... are you telling me you can breathe fire?"

He laughed. "No, not quite. I'm not entirely sure what I'm telling you. Maybe it's nothing at all, in fact. Just my imagination. When I was in the Grove, I didn't manage to do anything spectacular. But with practice..."

"With practice, maybe you'll find that you're able to do something incredible," I replied.

I hadn't given much thought to the fact that Callum had lost some of his power—some of what had always made him such a daunting presence when he walked into a room. Probably because he was no less daunting, no less impressive than he'd ever been. His power was simply redistributed now, into two separate bodies. Instead of turning into a dragon, he now rode one. He could still wield a sword or a crossbow like no one else.

And he still commanded the attention of everyone in a room, or out of it.

And in this moment, I was acutely aware that he still had the same incredible light blue eyes that had destroyed me the first time I'd looked up at his face.

Something told me that he and Caffall *separate* were an even more indomitable force than they had been as a single, unified entity.

"You'll be a good king," I said after a thoughtful pause. "The Crimson King was tormented by his dragon. You won't be. You'll be the first and only king of the Otherwhere who rides his dragon instead of being dominated by him. You and Caffall have a perfect relationship now. You're strong."

Callum let out a sad laugh.

"What is it?" I asked

"It's pretty ironic to think the very thing my family despised about me is now just…gone. I am no longer a dragon shifter. I'm simply a human."

"No," I said. "You're a dragon *lord*. That's not the same as a mere human."

"Dragon lord," he repeated with a grin. "I like the way those two words sound, coming from you." With that, he slipped his thumb over my lower lip, inspiring a reflexive smile. "If I become king, I'd like to be thought of that way."

"You will be king," I said. "The prophecy…"

Callum shook his head. "The prophecy states that the true heir will sit on the throne. It doesn't say my name. It could mean many things. Our demented friend Meligant may play a larger part in all this than we think."

"No way." I shook my head. "Everything else in the prophecy has come to pass, hasn't it? It's obvious that you're the one. You're the heir. You *have* to be."

"We'll see." Callum pulled me close, slipping a hand under my chin and whispering, "You know, I just remembered—we agreed that we weren't going to talk about all of this."

"Oops," I laughed, and, bowing my head, offered a quick flourish with my right hand. "Apologies…my King."

"Troublemaker," Callum said, silencing me by pressing his lips to mine.

MORNING

THAT NIGHT, we slept tangled in each other's arms, afraid to let go for fear that morning would come too soon.

When dawn finally broke through the large windows at the room's east end, I lay in bed, listening to the even rhythm of Callum's breaths.

An hour or more must have passed before I finally stretched and forced myself to get up and shower. I reconciled myself with the knowledge that I'd delayed as long as I could, and it was time to head back home to Fairhaven.

When we'd both dressed, Callum and I headed downstairs to the Great Hall, the enormous chamber where the Academy's residents dined, held meetings and assemblies, and even trained on rare occasions.

We spotted Lachlan sitting at a table on his own, seemingly deep in thought. But he smiled when he saw us, rising to his feet.

Taken aback, I stared at him for a few seconds. He seemed taller, somehow, and older than I remembered, despite the fact that I'd just seen him a day earlier.

"I'm going to head over and talk to Merriwether for a moment," Callum told me with a gentle hand to the small of my back. He nodded over to the far end of the Great Hall, where my grandfather was talking to Aithan, the Ranger I'd met in the North, and Niala, my closest friend at the Academy. "I'll be back."

With a nod and a smile, I headed over to Lachlan's table.

"You ready to head home?" he asked.

"Not really," I sighed, casting my eyes toward Callum. I knew Lachlan wasn't fond of being reminded of our relationship—of how deep my affection for Callum ran. But I wasn't about to censor myself to spare his feelings, either.

"Well, I suppose we have no choice," Lachlan said, his tone tinged with bitterness.

"True," I agreed. "The others want to get back to their homes. Meg, Olly, and Desmond are desperate to see their families, and I don't have the heart to ask them to stay here any longer."

"Families," Lachlan replied with a sad smile. "It must be nice to have people to look forward to."

He and I would not be returning to smiling parents, of course. No warm greetings, no hugs, no questions about our time in the Otherwhere or about the mundane aspects of our daily lives.

No questions about any of it.

Still, I wasn't worried that I'd feel alone when we returned, and I could only hope Lachlan wouldn't feel lonely, either.

"We do have family, you and I," I reminded him. "Liv, for one. Her parents have always looked after me like I was one of their own, and I'm sure they're fond of you, too."

"They're very good people," Lachlan agreed. "It's just…sometimes I wonder what life would've been like, if…"

"If you had a home like hers."

"Sure. Not that Waergs ever have cozy homes with welcome mats, picket fences, and rec rooms in the basement. Still, most of them have parents. I was raised in the woods by strangers."

I moved my eyes between him and Callum and realized for the first time that we were, each of us, orphaned in our way.

Lachlan had never known a true family. Callum's had rejected him.

And mine—the best, most loving parents anyone could ask for—had been taken from me years earlier, one horrible day.

"I'm sorry, Lachlan," I said. "Life's not fair, is it?"

"It is what it is," he replied with a shrug that was obviously meant to cover up his pain.

A second later, Desmond, Oleana, and Meg came charging into the Great Hall, running toward us with jubilant grins on their faces.

"We heard it's time!" Desmond sang. "We're really going home today?"

"We are," I replied.

"Amazing! Though I'm a little sad to go—your grandfather's been teaching me some amazing tricks, Vega!"

"Merriwether? Really? What sorts of tricks?"

"Magic. Sleight of hand," he said, balling his left hand into a fist, passing his right over it, then turning his left over to reveal a gold coin, the standard currency of the Otherwhere.

"I'm pretty sure that coin was in your hand the whole time, Des," Meg scoffed.

"I'm still working on it!" he snapped.

"No offense to this place," Meg said, ignoring him, "but I don't think I can take another day here. I'm chomping at the bit to get back to my mom's chicken pot pies."

"I get it," I laughed. "We all need to get on with our lives. But we need to remember that there's one more Relic of Power to find. Our job as Seekers isn't over. We may well be back this way soon."

"The Orb of Kilarin," Desmond sighed, looking around at the rest of us. "I keep forgetting about that one. Has anyone found any clues yet?"

I shook my head, Olly shrugged, and Meg simply chuckled.

"I've never once found a clue," she said. "I'm not as good at this whole Seeking business as some people."

"We're *all* good," I chastised, "which is why we've found three Relics. The fourth will show itself when it's ready. And don't forget, there are other Seekers out there. I'm sure they're eager to help. I'm not the only one who ever finds clues."

"You totally are," Oleana said. "At least, you're the only one who knows what to do when the clues show up. Without you, we wouldn't have found a single Relic."

"Well, maybe that's about to change."

"Nah. When all the Seekers get involved, it's way too many cooks in the kitchen," Desmond scoffed. "The last time we brought that many to find a Relic, we all came close to our bitter ends. One of us...*died*." The last word came out in a rasping, hesitant whisper.

"I remember," I said. "All too well."

"On a happier note," Oleana interjected semi-cheerfully, "Here's hoping we find the Orb soon. I'm about ready to settle back into a normal life without swords, daggers, freezing spells or wolf-men who want to shred my face into ground beef."

"Wolf-men, you say?" Lachlan replied with a smirk.

"Sorry. I forgot you're a Waerg."

"It's quite all right," he replied. "In my defense, I haven't ripped off that many faces."

"There's still time," Desmond said under his breath before adding, "I suppose we need to ask you to summon us up some doors, Vega. But we'll see you soon, yeah?"

"Hopefully not *too* soon," I replied with a grin. "Let's hope we can all have a nice, quiet Christmas without too much crazy thrown in."

"Here's hoping."

After a quick round of hugs, I summoned a Breach to each of my fellow Seekers' homes, sending them through before calling up a final one to Fairhaven.

"This one will take us straight to my house," I told Lachlan as I unlocked and opened the door. "You go first. I want to say goodbye to Callum."

"Of course," he said. "I'll see you in a minute."

I nodded. "In a minute."

I turned to face Callum, who had wandered over from the other end of the Great Hall. "Everything all right?"

"All good," he told me. "I was just watching all of you. You Seekers, you're like these walking balls of energy."

"I suppose," I said. "Maybe it comes from constantly looking for things. We're always on edge."

"That will end soon, at least." He scratched his jaw for a second before adding, "Lachlan has changed."

"Do you think so?"

He pulled his chin down. "You know so. There's something more mature about him. You see it, too. I know you do."

"I suppose," I replied. "I feel like something's on his mind. Maybe his latest brush with death made him rethink his life."

"Probably. My own brush with death certainly made me rethink mine. Just do him a favor and keep an eye on him, would you?"

"Of course," I said. "But not too close an eye. I wouldn't want to give him the wrong idea."

"Wrong idea?" Callum asked. "Ah. Yes. You don't want to lead him on." He took my hand and pulled it to his lips. "Poor Lachlan. It must be difficult for him."

"What must?"

"Being around you. I know it would be torture if I had to be close to you and couldn't kiss you."

"You seriously overestimate his feelings for me, Drake," I laughed. "We're just friends."

Though I wonder if Lachlan has come to accept that inconvenient fact yet...

"Of course."

Callum smiled, kissed me, his palms cupping my jaw, then pulled back.

"You need to get home and back to your life," he said.

"I will. But remember—I'm only ever a closed door away."

"I know," he said with a kiss to my cheek.

"We'll see each other in a few days."

"I know." A kiss to my forehead.

"I'll miss you."

"I know." This time, he brushed his lips against mine as he spoke, teasing me with the sensation I would miss most.

"I'll miss you too," he whispered. "More than you can possibly know."

BACK IN FAIRHAVEN

I'D ALL but forgotten that it would still be October in Fairhaven when I returned.

I'd barely made a dent in the school year. Yet so much had already happened since the first week of September.

When I'd left for the Otherwhere to retrieve the Lyre of Adair, I'd never anticipated the level of chaos the quest would unleash. I'd never suspected that I'd return to my hometown an utterly changed person.

A more powerful one, too.

I'd encountered a Coven of Witches. I'd learned of their magic, their lives, their ways. I'd also learned to harness my powers with a focus I didn't know I was capable of.

Not to mention that I was all but engaged to Callum now. The future king of the Otherwhere was one day—*possibly*—going to be my husband.

And my friendship with Lachlan, volatile though it was, was as solid and close as any I'd had in my entire life.

So it was with a good deal of sadness that I finally hugged him goodbye in my front hall.

"Well, Sloane," he said, running a hand through his mess of

dark curls and narrowing his striking green eyes at me, "it's been an adventure, hasn't it?"

"That's one word for it. It feels like we've been gone an entire year," I said, pulling my cell phone out of the bag on the console table by the front door. After clicking the side button to look at the time and date, I added, "but—oh, look—apparently we've been gone exactly twenty minutes."

"An eventful twenty minutes," Lachlan snickered. "I never thought I'd find myself riding a horse across the Otherwhere. Of course, I never thought I'd find myself in the care of a Coven of Witches, either. That was probably the most surprising bit. I wish I'd been able to get to know them better…but it's a little hard when you're largely unconscious."

"To think you were so untrusting of them at first," I laughed. "Then again, so was I. They turned out to be quite different from what we both expected."

"They have a way of growing on one, don't they?" he replied, his tone pensive, his gaze suddenly distant. "It's almost like…"

"Like what?"

"It's hard to put into words," he said with a shake of his head. "It's just…when I was in the infirmary in Aradia recovering from my wounds, I felt…"

"You felt…?"

He bit his lip, shook his head, and said, "Nothing. It's not important. Listen, I'll head out now, and let you get some rest before school starts up again. I'm sure you could use a little relaxation time."

"Yeah, I could."

But as he turned away, I stopped him.

"Lachlan…"

He spun back to face me, but I was barely able to look into his emerald-colored eyes.

"Yes?" he said, his tone a little too enthusiastic for my taste.

"I can't tell you…" I said, the sound of my voice trailing off as I lost my nerve.

"It's all right. You don't have to say anything. We've been through a lot together, and I get it."

"It's just…I appreciate everything you've done so much. I hope you know that."

"You're acting like we'll never see each other again. Like there's not another Relic to find, or a war to fight after that, Vega. It's not like this is over. We'll be in one another's lives for some time, fighting on the same side of this long battle."

"Well, in the meantime, I'm going to have to try and put it out of my mind while I focus on school and grades and stuff. "

"Grades? You're talking like someone who's planning to head to university next year."

"Why shouldn't I?" I asked. "I mean, it's a possibility, right?"

Lachlan ground his jaw for a second before saying, "It's just… Niala mentioned that she thought maybe you and Callum were planning to…stay together. Permanently."

"Ah," I said with a slightly uncomfortable smirk. "That."

"It's okay. I'm happy for you—really, I am. I guess I'm just confused about the timeline. So, you're planning on finishing senior year?"

"I'm only seventeen, Lachlan. I'll turn eighteen in the summer. I have a long life ahead of me—assuming I don't get myself killed in the near future. I want to enjoy some of what this world has to offer before I commit to living in another one…regardless of how much I love Callum. He understands that. Besides, I don't want to be a high school dropout. My parents would have hated that. They did everything they could to give Will and me good lives, and Will has sacrificed so much for me. I can't let him down."

"Are you sure there isn't a little more to it than that?"

"More? Like what?"

"Come on. What girl in her right mind would hesitate to commit to the great Callum Drake?"

"I'm not hesitating," I snapped. "That's not what this is."

"Right. You love him so much that you're talking about a possible future without him."

"It's not that simple," I said, my voice tightening.

I wanted to yell at him, to tell him he didn't understand.

The truth was, *I* was the one who didn't understand. I did love Callum with all my heart. I never, ever wanted to lose him.

But I couldn't quite seem to accept that maybe, just maybe, I could leave my world and my life behind.

"Look—just let me focus on school," I said after a deep breath. "The rest will sort itself out."

"Okay. I promise I'll needle you about your grades, if you like. I can be like the annoying little demon on your shoulder, telling you to study instead of playing some exploding candy game on your phone all the time."

"Wouldn't you be the *angel* on my shoulder? The demon would be the one trying to tempt me into doing bad things."

"I suppose, but angels seem a little dull. I'd rather carry a tiny pitchfork and poke your earlobe now and then while I whisper, 'Psst, Vega…Finish your Ode to a Belgian Waffle in Iambic Pentameter! Write an essay on the tragic equine casualties of the Civil War!'"

"Great," I laughed. "Just what every girl wants. A nagging little smartass in her ear."

"I aim to be useful."

"Thanks. Now, go home so I can rest, you pushy weirdo."

I gave him one final hug before yanking the door open, only to hear a familiar voice bellow, "What the hell is going on here?"

LIFE

Liv was standing on my porch, her hand in the air as if she was about to knock.

As she assessed the scene before her, her expression morphed from surprise to horror, and I could only imagine the paranoid-teenage-girl-scenario that was doubtless racing through her mind.

"Liv!" I shouted, resisting the temptation to throw my arms around her. After all, as far as she knew, we'd been together in school only a little while earlier.

"What's going on?" she asked, her voice as tight as a freshly braided rope. "Why are you two here...together? I thought...I mean...not that I have a problem with it or anything, but..."

My throat went dry as I struggled to come up with a response that would make any sense at all.

"I...we..." I began, but words failed me.

"I...couldn't find my English binder," Lachlan quickly blurted out, "in my bag, and remembered that Vega and I both have gray ones, so I thought maybe she'd picked mine up by accident."

"Yes!" I said, quickly blinking my eyes shut to summon a dark gray binder on the console table underneath the front hall's large mirror. Trying to conceal my trembling hands, I picked it up and handed it to Lachlan. "Sorry about that. I totally thought it was mine."

"Right," he replied, grabbing the binder before wrapping Liv in a surprising bear hug that instantly seemed to make all her suspicion melt away. "Liv," he said cheerfully, "would you like to do something tonight? Just you and me?"

"Really?" she asked, her voice a virtual squeal.

"Really."

"Oh my God, yes!"

Lachlan turned to me, his eyes flashing bright for just a second before fading again. "Thanks for the binder," he said, holding it up. "I really thought I was screwed without my notes."

"No problem." I smiled at him as he slipped an arm around Liv and escorted her off the porch. She turned and shot me a wide-eyed look of blissful wonder as she slipped her arm around Lachlan's waist.

"We're going on a date!" she mouthed percussively.

I gave her the thumbs up then shut the door, pressing my back to it and letting out the hugest sigh of my entire freaking life.

THE NEXT SEVERAL weeks were surprisingly normal.

Sort of.

I managed to focus on my schoolwork and to avoid the Charmers—my ubiquitous, nasty trio of high school tormentors —for the most part, though Miranda threw me occasional biting questions about Callum's whereabouts. Everyone had noticed his disappearance, of course; after all, he had a reputation as Plymouth High's most handsome male student, and his absence had left something of a void—though I had noticed certain girls paying more attention to Lachlan than usual.

More than once, Miranda told me she was certain Callum had disappeared because I was such an atrocious girlfriend that he couldn't stand being in the same town as me, let alone the same school.

Tempting though it was to summon a pair of razor-sharp scissors and slice off clumps of her perfect, silk-smooth hair, I simply smiled and told her Callum was on a top-secret mission to rid the world of bitchy teenage girls by any means possible.

It was enough to shut her up for a time.

I attended my classes, as always. In English, Lachlan and I exchanged the occasional knowing glance as our teacher delved into talk of Arthurian tales and asked us to write a short story depicting knights, dragons, and adventure.

I considered writing a semi-autobiographical version of the last few weeks of my life, but was convinced the teacher would flag it as absurd and give me a giant red F, with the note:

Come on, Vega. A golden dragon, severed from its human half? A Usurper Queen? An evil wizard? This delves beyond cliché into absolute madness.
See me after class.

Ms. Maddox—the awful, light-haired Waerg whose pack had raised Lachlan, and who taught Chemistry at Plymouth High— snarled at me occasionally when I passed her in the hallway.

But I no longer feared her. She was a gnat, a parasite, something that would go away if I ignored it long enough. She was a servant of the Usurper Queen, and I told myself nothing she could do would be enough to keep me from hunting for the final Relic.

Just for fun, one day as I was walking by her, I tested a theory.

Solara had told me that if I learned to harness my gifts, I might be able to cast the same spells that she and other Witches could. I hadn't entirely believed her, but something about

Maddox's presence that afternoon was enough to prompt me into action.

When she and I were within a few feet of one another, I closed my eyes and mouthed the words "Tempo cessat…"

When I opened my eyes, Maddox and I were standing two feet apart, and the students around us were frozen. The spell, it seemed, had worked like a charm. I'd stopped time for all but the two of us.

But the icing on the cake was the dagger that hung in the air mere inches from Maddox's stern face, its tip pointed straight at her.

A smile formed on my lips as Maddox's eyes widened with both fear and what actually looked like bewildered awe.

The students around us, oblivious to the altercation, remained still as rock-hard statues even as the dagger moved slowly toward Maddox's nose, threatening to pierce her flesh. She crossed her eyes comically as she attempted to track the weapon's trajectory.

"Your skills have improved, Seeker," she half-hissed, tightening. "I'm impressed."

"You think?" I replied, stepping toward her, flicking my hand in the air and erasing the dagger from existence. "Gee, thanks. Your approval means so much to me."

"Doesn't matter. You still aren't strong enough to defeat Lumus," she growled under her breath. "Nor are you strong enough to take on the Mistress. When the time comes, they will crush you and that Headmaster grandfather of yours, not to mention your Severed boyfriend. I've heard he's weak now. A mere man, and nothing more."

"You know perfectly well that I can take on the queen," I sneered. "I've done it before, and I'm much stronger now than I was then. And you're wrong about Callum. He's no ordinary man."

I said the last few words with an abundance of confidence,

though I wasn't *entirely* sure I was right. Callum hadn't told me anything about what he'd done when I was off visiting Solara. Only that he'd "tested a theory." That could have meant anything.

Maddox grinned. "You haven't seen what the Mistress has been working on. You have no idea what she's truly capable of."

"I know she's a walking dumpster fire, and that's all I need to know," I said, walking on as I released my fellow students from the Time-Stop spell.

"There's something else you don't know," Maddox snapped. "Something that will destroy any plans you may have for a happily ever after."

I spun around and said, "Oh? What's that?"

But instead of explaining, she simply narrowed her eyes, smiled a toothy, menacing grin, and walked away.

THANKSGIVING

Each Friday evening, I summoned a Breach to the Academy to visit Callum. We'd agreed before my departure that seeing one another once a week was just enough to keep us both satisfied without eating into the time I needed to study. Or that he needed to train, consult with Merriwether about the coming war, or go out on surveillance flights with Caffall.

He always held me as I fell asleep, though I often woke in the mornings in my own room, never quite remembering how I'd found my way home.

Never did more than a week pass without us seeing one another. We'd lost too much time already, during the time when he'd been in a comatose state, lingering somewhere near death.

One night in early November, as he lay with his arm draped over me, I hesitated, then brought up a topic I'd been pondering for some time.

"I know you don't like being away from Caffall," I said, "but I'm wondering about something."

"What is it?"

"Well, Christmas is coming soon. Will's going to be coming back to Fairhaven for a few days, and I'd really love for you to meet him properly. Obviously I can't exactly bring him here to meet you, so I thought maybe…"

"Ah," Callum replied. I could hear a smile in that one syllable. "You want me to meet your famous brother. I have to admit, I'm a little afraid to find myself face to face with him."

"You, afraid?" I laughed. "Why?"

"He's your big brother. Big brothers are highly intimidating."

"He's, like, a hundred years younger than you. And he definitely doesn't know how to wield a sword or crossbow, let alone fly a dragon around. He shouldn't intimidate you in the least."

"Still…some things transcend brute force, Vega."

"You haven't answered my question, Callum. Will you come on Christmas Eve?"

"I'll tell you what—find a way to conjure a snowstorm on Christmas Eve, and I would be glad to come."

"A snowstorm?" I laughed.

"I'm serious. It would be helpful. I'd need to bring Caffall with me, and I'd want to hide him from watchful eyes. A snowstorm keeps people from spotting him."

"But people in my world aren't supposed to be able to see dragons," I protested. "They're…immune to magic, or whatever."

"They're not entirely immune," Callum said. "And believe me, they'll notice a giant golden dragon circling above the town, if he's too visible."

"Okay. I'll see what I can do," I said with a wink. "But I'm not exactly the sort of spell-caster who controls the weather. I'm not Solara. I'm still learning the basics."

"You might surprise yourself one of these days, Sloane."

"So people have been telling me for months. You all have too much faith in me."

"You have too little in yourself. Now let's go to sleep and have some nice dreams about Christmas when the snow will fall, your brother and I will meet, and all will be perfect."

"Deal."

I fell asleep happy that night. Excited by the prospect of my brother meeting the boy I loved. Excited by the future and all that it might hold.

But most of all, I was excited about the prospect of having Callum back in Fairhaven with me, even for a day or two.

That alone would be enough to make it the best Christmas I'd had in a long, long time.

THANKSGIVING CAME in a mostly cheerful flurry of activity.

Decaying leaves lay in a colorful patchwork on the ground outside, a crisp carpet to tread through with satisfying kicks of boot-clad feet as I made my way to Liv's house for dinner with her family. Lachlan, who had also been invited, spent the evening looking slightly awkward and uncomfortable as Liv kept one arm locked firmly around his shoulder, as if laying claim to him.

I couldn't help but laugh internally to look at them. Liv was still as smitten as ever. Lachlan, on the other hand, seemed a little lost, clearly hesitant to commit to her in any way, and generally ill at ease.

They did make a cute, if confusing, couple.

I found myself stuffed, grateful for the hospitality, and very relaxed by the time dessert was served, appreciating the fact that I still had a sort-of-family to keep me from missing Will and otherwise feeling lonely on an occasion normally reserved for large family gatherings.

After we'd managed to devour most of an enormous pumpkin pie, I offered to help clear the table. Liv's mother, who'd always doted on me like I was made of fragile crystal, shooed me away with a wave of her hand, and I surrendered, wandering out to the back deck to get a breath of fresh air.

Lachlan came out to join me while Liv and her mother loaded the dishwasher.

I leaned against the railing and looked out toward the woods that surrounded Fairhaven, breathing in chilly air and grinning into the night.

"Life feels so normal right now, doesn't it?" I said. "I mean, in a good way."

"Yes, very," he replied. "Very normal."

But he didn't sound quite as content as I felt.

"What is it?"

He sighed, pressing his elbows against the railing, and looked down at the ground below. "I've been missing the idea of family lately—even though I never really had one. I mean, I had Maddox and the Pack for years, but she was a drill sergeant, as you can imagine. Not exactly a mother figure. And now, she's my enemy." He turned to me, his eyes bright in the darkness. "We used to hunt in these woods on Thanksgiving each year, you know. We'd chase down rabbits, deer, you name it, and we'd feast. It wasn't exactly sitting around a table with a roast turkey, but it was still a tradition. And now, I have to admit that I'm feeling a little lost."

"Right," I said. "I know that feeling. But remember, you do have us. Liv and me. Maybe we can start some new traditions that don't involve quite so much carnage."

"Maybe," he smirked. "Thanks. But I have to admit, that's not the only reason I'm feeling very self-pitying tonight."

"What is it, then?"

"Can you keep a secret?"

I put my hands on my waist and fake-glared at him. "Am I a Seeker who travels to the Otherwhere through magical doors that I summon with nothing but my mind?"

Lachlan laughed. "Okay, fair enough."

"So, tell me!"

He winced. "I turned eighteen recently. I wasn't going to tell anyone, but…"

"What? When?"

"Maddox told me when I was a kid that my birthday was October fifth."

"That was weeks ago!" I said, slapping his arm. "How could you not tell us? We could have done something for you! A cake, at the very least."

"I didn't want to make a big deal of it. I figured it would come and go, and that would be that. Thing is, though, I…I don't know, it's like I feel *different*, somehow. And I haven't been able to talk to Liv about it, for obvious reasons."

I pulled away and looked at him. "I thought there was something going on with you. It felt like something changed after you recovered in the Otherwhere. You seemed more mature, or older, or…I don't know. Like you turned into an adult while I remained a teenager."

He nodded. "Maybe it doesn't mean anything," he said. "It could just be my brain, telling me I'm different now. It's just a number, really."

"Your wolf," I said, "does *he* feel different to you?"

I realized then that I hadn't seen Lachlan's wolf in ages. I'd spent nights curled up next to him in the Otherwhere—cold nights when we were traveling toward the mountains. He'd defended me in the woods, when our enemies had attacked.

But I hadn't laid eyes on him since.

We'd never talked about the gray wolf much. Not like Callum and I talked about Caffall. It was like he was some distant part of Lachlan, a shadow that lingered just behind him, yet wasn't entirely attached.

I'd always assumed it was because their relationship was different, less fraught than Callum's with Caffall. Lachlan had always seemed so in control, so calm and calculating, whereas Callum had always had an edge to him, like there was a quiet rage brewing just beneath the surface of his skin.

"Not different, exactly," Lachlan said. "It's more that he and I feel…I don't know, incomplete. Like there's something out there

55

we need. Something we crave. But the frustrating thing is, I don't know what."

"I see. It seems you're having a mid-life crisis," I said with a chuckle.

"If this is mid-life, I must not be planning to live very long."

"Fine, then. A *young adult* crisis. Anyhow, I'm sure it's fine, whatever it is. *You're* fine. Look, it's senior year. We're all trying to figure out what to do with ourselves after high school's over. Everyone's lost and confused, but we all walk around pretending to have our heads on straight. But the truth is, we're all a bunch of insecure, baffled almost-adults."

Lachlan shrugged. "Right. Maybe that's all it is."

"What are you two talking about?" Liv's voice chirped from behind us. Lachlan and I exchanged a quick *How long has she been listening?* look before turning to smile at her.

"Vega thinks I'm having a mid-life crisis," Lachlan told her.

"No way," Liv replied. "You have decades ahead of you before that happens. You're probably just suffering a bout of quiet emotional torment because you haven't asked me on a date in weeks." She skipped over and took him by the arm. "Poor thing, it must be eating away at you."

"Right," he said, his body stiffening visibly. "That must be it."

"It's all right," Liv giggled. "You don't have to. Just promise me you'll reserve New Year's Eve for me, would you? I need someone to kiss."

Lachlan tossed me a quick *Help me!* glance before saying, "Um…I'll keep that in mind, Liv."

"Good. Now come in and help me finish cleaning up, would you? We can leave Vega out here to stare at the stars, or whatever it is that she does when no one's looking."

I watched them walk into the house, exhaling a cloud of vapor into the chilly evening air as I recalled the one kiss I'd shared with Lachlan.

Maybe it was guilt that made me decide then and there that tonight would be an excellent time for a surprise visit to Callum.

SEVERAL HOURS LATER, after a long, pleasurable visit capped off by Callum falling asleep next to me, my thoughts turned to Meligant for the first time in what felt like weeks.

There had been no talk of him in ages. No talk of the frightening silver dragon or of the son Meligant claimed to seek. But as I struggled against insomnia, the mystery of his long-lost child insisted on working its way through my mind like a puzzle I desperately needed to solve.

After a few hours of restless tossing and turning, I finally rose from the bed and pulled on my sweater, which was draped over a nearby chair.

"Going somewhere?" Callum asked, groggily turning over to watch me.

"Back home," I told him with an apologetic smile. "There's something I need to do."

"Uh-oh. *Something I need to do* are words that always seem to lead to chaos. Unless…" he propped himself on his elbows, his muscles taut. "Have you found a hint to the Orb of Kilarin's location?"

"No, nothing like that," I replied. "But since you mention it, I do want to go on a little hunt."

"A hunt."

"I'm a Seeker, after all. It's what I do."

"It's very hard for me to sit here, hear those words, and not quietly freak out." Callum cocked his head to the side and threw me a dubious glance. "Whatever you're about to do, just promise me you'll be careful."

"Of course."

"Promise me you won't do anything reckless."

"Of course."

"Promise me you won't do anything I wouldn't do."

At that, my smile grew, I stepped over and leaned down to kiss him, and told him I'd be back to visit soon.

"I honestly don't know what I'll find, if anything," I said. "Or if I'll succeed in my self-inflicted mission—and end up dead."

"That's it. I'm coming with you," he said, tearing the covers off and swinging his legs around to climb out of bed. "I can bring Caffall. I can—"

"You can go back to sleep. I was kidding—I won't die. I promise."

"Fine." With a sigh, he replied, "You've trusted your instincts this long and you're still alive. Here's hoping your streak continues."

He rose to his feet as I conjured the door into my bedroom back home in Fairhaven. When I'd stepped through and turned to watch the door vanish, Callum was standing, shirtless, in the white bedroom in the Rose Wing of the Academy, a grin on his face that made me want to leap back through and give him one last lingering kiss.

But the door vanished and I exhaled, steeling myself for the task ahead.

A HUNT

From my bedroom in Fairhaven I could see the sun lingering just over the horizon, a broad, blazing disc of the purest orange. The day looked to be cloudless, if a little chilly.

I headed downstairs to the kitchen, prepared a pot of coffee, and contemplated my next move.

I found myself mulling over what Solara had told me about the child, searching for clues among her words.

It had happened decades ago. He could be any age. He might live anywhere in this world or the Otherwhere.

But something—a feeling, a tiny voice somewhere deep inside my mind—told me he was close.

And I intended to find him, if only to make sure he was safely beyond Meligant's reach.

On a whim, I called up a Breach to a place I'd been once before—a small, quaint shop nestled in the center of the isolated, somewhat hostile town of Volkston in the Otherwhere. It was a place populated by Waergs and Grells, neither of whom was particularly fond of human visitors.

I stepped through the summoned door into the frigid air of the Otherwhere, drawing the confused gazes of a couple of Grells headed toward me. One of them, a woman with the piercing blue eyes of a Husky, glared at me, and I was certain that I heard her mutter something to her companion about Witches.

I turned away and marched over to the shop's front door, pushing it open and heading in. A woman with jet black hair turned my way, her amber eyes and feline features morphing into a not entirely friendly smile.

"We meet again, Vega Sloane," she said. "I must say, I did not anticipate a visit."

"I thought you anticipated everything, Mareya," I said, my tone admittedly a little chilly.

"It would take a fool to assume you'd ever return to my shop. As I recall, I am not your favorite person in the Otherwhere."

"To be fair, the last time I saw your face, I was convinced you'd just tried to burn my friend and me alive."

"But you know better now."

I nodded. "Yes, I do. I know you were trying to help us. I appreciate it, and I'm sorry for misjudging you."

I turned to peruse the trinkets in her shop—the strangely shaped skulls, the multicolored vials of potion, the exquisite books of different sizes that lined the shelves.

I no longer felt the same fear I had the first time I'd visited. The place was beginning to seem more like home than like enemy territory.

"What can I do for you?" she asked. "Surely you're not here to find another map?"

I chuckled. "No, definitely not. I've come because…" I began, quickly realizing I wasn't quite sure how to complete the sentence. "I'm…looking for someone. The thing is, I'm not sure who she is. Or where she is. Or even *when* she is."

"Ah. I see." Mareya leaned back against the counter, crossed her arms, and stared at me with an amused, knowing grin.

"Okay, well," I said, "you didn't tell me I'm nuts, so that's a good start."

"You're seeking a Witch."

I opened my mouth to ask how she could possibly know that, but shut it again and finally said, "Yes, I am."

"What is her name?"

"Suspiria."

"Suspiria…" Mareya said slowly, tasting the syllables on her tongue. "I remember hearing of her—an impressive talent, she was. Part of the Marigni Coven. Suspiria has not been seen in the Otherwhere for many years. They say she disappeared without a trace decades ago."

"But you know who she is?"

"I know of every Witch who has ever dwelt within our borders." Mareya eyed me curiously, stepping forward. "But she is not the only one you seek, is she?"

"I don't know what you mean," I lied. I'd never entirely trusted Mareya. But more than anything, I didn't want to find myself responsible for giving away Solara's family secret.

Then again, Mareya probably already knew.

"No matter. If it's the Witch you want, I will do what I can to assist you." Mareya turned away and, without a word, strode through a set of curtains into the shop's back room. She returned a few seconds later, holding an object wrapped in red silk.

"A Seer's Stone," she told me as she set the object down on the counter between us and the silk fell away to reveal a smooth glass sphere. "There are many in the Otherwhere and in your world. But the most powerful of them, of course, is one you've seen before."

"The Orb of Kilarin," I said. "The last of the Four Relics of Power. Yes, I've seen it more than once, but it faded from the Academy some time ago."

"As you know, the person in possession of the Orb can see great distances over time and space. The Orb allows one to find any person, any creature their heart or mind desires, regardless of where—or when—they may exist. If you possessed the Orb of Kilarin and wished to watch an ancestor of yours working in their garden hundreds of years ago, it would allow you to do so."

"I didn't know that," I said. "Will that work for just anyone?"

Mareya shook her head. "Only for the powerful. You, Vega, would be able to harness its power, but a human from your world —one without magical blood—could not. It is what makes the Orb so important and so dangerous at once. I fear it's found its way into the wrong hands."

"You think someone's found it? A Seeker?"

"I didn't say that. Only that its resting place—its *hiding* place— is somewhere quite dangerous."

"Every Relic so far has found its way to somewhere danger-ous," I scowled. "It's like they're *trying* to kill us."

Mareya laughed. "I suppose you could look at it that way. Or you could say they're protecting themselves."

I eyed the Seer's stone. "Are you telling me you don't know where this Suspiria person is?" I asked. "That you can't find her?"

"I can find her," she told me. "Though I am not sure you'll like what you discover, Seeker. Secrets exist for a reason—and some-times that reason isn't clear until it's too late."

"I'm willing to take the risk," I replied, gritting my teeth at Mareya's typically cryptic words. "Look, I don't think it matters whether I like what I discover or not. I'm trying to protect some-one. A *lot* of someones, actually. It's important that I learn the truth."

"Perhaps the best way to protect those people is to leave the past alone," Mareya said with a sigh, passing a hand over the smooth sphere as she stared into its depths. "The stone is telling me the same."

"I don't care what the stone says," I told her. "This is important."

Mareya's shoulders hunched as if she was deflating, then she straightened once again, pulling her eyes to mine.

"If you must search for Suspiria, look for her in the Witch Town."

"Witch Town?" I asked. "You mean Aradia?"

She shook her head. "Much closer to home than that, Vega Sloane."

With that, a high-pitched ringing echoed through the shop, and I turned to see that two clients—a Grell and a Waerg, both of whom eyed me with looks of serious hostility—had just wandered in.

"Be careful, Seeker," Mareya told me quietly, reaching up and grabbing a thick book from the shelf to her right. "Learn what you can. Prepare yourself for what is to come. There may be no Witches around to help you when the time comes to fight for your life and those around you."

As she handed the book to me, I read its title.

Advanced Sorcery for the Highly Gifted.

"What's this?" I asked.

"A book."

"I can see that," I replied, only to see that Mareya's lips were teasing their way into an amused grin. "Why are you giving it to *me?*"

"Because you're ready for the next phase in your evolution, Sorcière. It's time you learned what you're truly capable of."

Sorcière.

Merriwether had once called me the same thing. He'd told me I had the potential to develop into a powerful Sorceress—that my bloodline would lead me to skills I'd never known I possessed.

But I couldn't say I'd taken my grandfather entirely seriously. I didn't feel all that different now than I had a few months earlier. I'd cast one truly impressive spell—the Melding that had brought Callum back from the brink of death—but that was with the guidance of Solara, and the help of the Scepter of Morgana.

My meager ability to conjure food and drink wouldn't help in the war to come, unless we planned on flinging sausages at our enemies.

"You really want me to read this?" I asked, turning the huge tome over in my hands. It must have been a thousand pages long, and it felt like it weighed at least ten pounds.

Mareya shook her head. "You don't need to read it. Not exactly. You may find that its contents are easier to absorb than you think. Have some faith, Vega Sloane. If not in yourself, then in me."

"Well…thank you, I think," I replied, recalling that the last time I'd held a book in Mareya's shop, she'd charged me fifty gold coins for one torn-out page. "I'll do as you suggest, though I still don't think I'm the all-powerful being everyone seems to think I am. I feel like you all have it backwards."

"No one is all-powerful. But you are very strong. There is a fire in you that I saw the first time I laid eyes on you, my girl."

My girl.

Two strangely familiar words.

On the day of my parents' funeral, my Nana put an arm around me and said, "It's all right to cry, my girl. You must allow yourself to break down, so that you can build yourself up once again."

I stared at Mareya, an odd, familiar feeling sending a shot of warmth through my bloodstream. I'd always felt wary of the Witch, like she was playing with me in vaguely malicious ways. But in that moment, I felt oddly close to her.

Then again, Mareya was no Nana.

"Still," she continued, "the days to come will test you. So you need to develop your powers. Harness what lies within you. You will need every ounce of your strength. You will need a strong heart, as it, too, will be tested."

"I'm not entirely sure what you're talking about," I said, "but I'll do my best."

"I know you will."

I was about to turn away when I stopped and asked, "Has anyone ever told you you'd be a lot more helpful if you didn't talk in half-riddles all the time?"

Mareya clicked her tongue against her teeth and grinned. "Where would be the fun in that?"

When she laughed and walked away to greet her other clients, I ducked into the back room to summon a Breach to Fairhaven.

THE BOOK OF SPELLS

WHEN I STEPPED in my bedroom, I set the book Mareya had given me aside. I was suddenly exhausted, as if my brief visit had taken a great deal out of me.

Maybe my lingering wish to uncover the truth was proving too much for me. I was torn up inside, as if I had two conflicting voices both pleading with me at the same time.

One begged me to continue the search.

The other told me to stop before I went too far.

Both voices warned of dire consequences, either for my action or my inaction.

As I contemplated my dilemma, Merriwether's words of caution wove their way through my mind once again:

Be careful what you wish for.

"Right," I said out loud. "Maybe instead of thinking too hard about any of this, I should just relax."

I headed downstairs, plopped down on the couch, and turned the television on. For some less than sane reason, I decided to watch a movie about a serial killer who targeted young women who lived alone.

This is a hell of a way to spend my Thanksgiving weekend, I muttered to myself.

THE FOLLOWING WEEK, I found myself back in my classes at Plymouth High, back to my banal but pleasant existence. Back to handing in hastily-drafted essays, scrambling to complete copious amounts of homework, and back to fluttery anticipation of my Friday night visits to Callum.

For a few days, I even managed to keep my mind off my unsuccessful hunt, focusing instead on the assignments that were due before Christmas. A History project. A French presentation. A sonnet for Creative Writing class.

By the time Friday rolled around, I was filled with both a sense of accomplishment and the feeling that I'd been wearing blinders all week, denying a reality that I couldn't fully escape.

And, happy though I was to lay eyes on Callum when I stepped through a Breach into the Otherwhere, I seemed incapable of hiding my preoccupation from him.

"Something's going on with you," he told me when I arrived in the Academy's Rose Wing on Friday evening. "What is it?"

"Nothing," I half-lied as I smiled up at him, my hands grabbing at his shirt to pull him close. "I'm probably just tired from thinking ahead to Christmas and what I need to do to prepare. It's the first year I've gotten ready for the holidays without Will around to guide me. It's taking a lot of mental energy."

"I'm not convinced that's all that's on your mind." With a calming kiss to my neck, he added, "But remember, you have Liv. And Lachlan. I'm sure they'd be happy to help."

I smirked. "I don't want to put them out. They have their own stuff going on."

The truth was, I'd been avoiding close contact with Lachlan since our conversation at Liv's on Thanksgiving.

I'd enjoyed the chat, of course, and I appreciated the trust he'd put in me.

But every time I looked into his eyes, I was reminded of our journey together through the Otherwhere. His declarations of powerful feelings for me...

And the kiss that should never have happened.

He was a source of joy and guilt at once. A walking tower of confusion.

I cared about him, of course.

But I was in love with Callum—*he* was everything to me. He was the very reason I'd risked my life trekking through the Otherwhere in the first place.

The problem was, somewhere along the way, I'd hurt Lachlan. Maybe it wasn't entirely my fault—I'd tried at every turn not to lead him on. But I couldn't deny how much I cared for him, and maybe I'd given him false hope that my feelings translated into something more intense than friendship.

Then again, maybe I was overthinking everything, as usual.

"I'm actually quite happy to prepare for the holiday on my own," I assured Callum. "I guess I'm just a little nervous. I'm really looking forward to your visit. I want so badly for you and Will to meet, to get along. You're the two most important men in my life."

"Ah, yes," he said. "The much-anticipated meeting of two males who will inevitably end up battling it out tacitly for your affection. We'll see. You still have to work on your snowstorm skills, Sloane."

"You're really serious about that, huh?"

"Not entirely," he chuckled. "Truth be told, I'll find a way to come to Fairhaven even without a storm. I'm sure Caffall could hide himself away, if it came down to it. The woods in that region are dense, and he's adept at concealment, as all dragons are."

"Well, hopefully it won't come to that. I'll put a call in to the weather gods and see what I can do."

"Good," Callum said, stifling a yawn. Whatever he'd been up to all week had exhausted him, it seemed. So I led him to the bed, lay down next to him, tucked my face against his chest...and listened as his deep breath evolved into the contented purr of deep, blissful sleep.

WHEN I WAS BACK in my room in Fairhaven the next day, I finally cracked open the massive book Mareya had given me.

At its front was a table of contents, listing a series of chapters on topics like Mental Focus for Magic Users, Spell-casting, Healing, Conjuring, and other magical abilities I'd encountered over my months in the Otherwhere.

One chapter was called "About Time," and included Temporal Spells like the one I'd used on Maddox in the school's hallway.

It also talked about the rare talent that Suspiria had for creating Temporal Portals to different eras, past and future. The book offered no instructions for the spell. Instead, it simply described the skill as "not without risk," and explained that one could easily change the course of history if one chose to abuse the ability.

No kidding.

I kept perusing the book, my interest piquing at a chapter on "Forgetting Spells," which were useful when it came to Worlders —the people who lived in my world—witnessing magic they were never supposed to see.

One paragraph described a spell called *Induced Amnesia*. It was a verbal incantation for use on large crowds in public places.

I mouthed the words, committing them to memory:

Conoit destruit.

The book claimed that a spell-caster could choose to exclude specific people from the effects by touching them before conjuring the spell.

Moving on, I flipped to a chapter on offensive spells, which included the creation of Fireballs, Ice Missiles, and various forms of Mind Control, though the book did caution that not all magic users would be able to cast such a broad array of attacks.

"Sorcery relies upon the development of elemental skills," the text read. "Those with ice coursing through their blood are adept with Chill Spells. There are Witches, wizards, warlocks and others capable of Air, Water, and Fire spells, as well. It is up to the student to experiment. But be warned: personal injury can, and probably will, occur."

"Don't I know it," I muttered.

I stared at a few of the images painted on the book's pages. A hand hurling a fireball. A Witch summoning a lightning storm.

The chapter continued by talking about the control of objects with one's mind. Pathics, like Freya, the Seeker Candidate who'd once tried to assassinate me, could hurl anything from rocks to tree trunks with nothing more than a thought.

I'd managed such a spell with the knife I'd used to threaten Maddox. But I'd never actually hurled a weapon with my mind.

Closing my eyes, I told myself to summon something small and simple. "A rock," I said. "A small one. Floating in the air."

I opened my eyes to see a fist-sized stone, rotating slowly in the middle of my room as if awaiting my command. It was gray and unremarkable, though it looked like it could definitely blacken someone's eye if called upon to do so.

Mouthing the word "Fly," I winced, waiting for something to happen, before opening my eyes again.

The stone simply dropped to the floor with a loud thud.

I laughed at myself. "Merriwether was wrong. I'm no Sorcière," I said. "I summoned a rock, and that rock discovered gravity."

I was about to give up when I found myself picturing my brother's deep voice inside my mind, chastising me for doubting myself like I always did. "Come on, Vega. Don't settle for mediocrity. Don't give up so quickly, or you'll never know what you can accomplish."

I stretched my hand out, pointing a finger toward the stone, and, in an assertive voice, said, "Rise."

The rock obeyed, levitating until it hovered once again in mid-air, awaiting my next move.

Narrowing my eyes at the small weapon, I once again whispered, "Fly."

This time, the rock did exactly as I asked, hurtling toward the window with all the horrifying speed of a baseball flung by a professional pitcher.

"Oh, crap! *Tempo cessat!*" I yelled, but I was too late. The rock had already shot through one of the window's panes, leaving a jagged, gaping hole behind.

"Okay, maybe hurling conjured blunt objects is not the best thing to practice indoors," I laughed, cursing myself for my clumsiness.

When I'd patched up the window with some duct tape and cardboard, I decided to set the book aside for a little. Best not to tempt fate. Much as I wanted to learn, I'd probably end up destroying the house if I tried too much at once.

What I should really look for is a chapter on getting my room to clean itself...

I lay down on my bed and stared at the ceiling, contemplating what Mareya had said to me. *Harness what lies within you. You will need every ounce of your strength in the days to come.*

How the hell was I supposed to know what lies within me?

In my time at the Academy I'd met Healers, Sparker, Pathics, Diggers, who controlled people's minds, and others. But never had I met someone who was capable of a whole array of spells until I met the Witches of Aradia.

Unless, of course, I counted my grandfather.

Merriwether was always subtle in his spell-casting. He could open doors with nothing more than a twitch of his fingers. He had the uncanny ability to see into the future, just as some Witches could. All without the use of a Seer's stone.

But I had no real idea just how gifted he might truly be.

And I wasn't sure I ever wanted to learn the extent of his powers.

The truth was, I wasn't even sure I wanted to learn the extent of my own.

CHARMING

On the Monday morning two weeks after Thanksgiving, I found myself standing by my locker with Liv.

"What did you do this weekend?" she asked, angling her head to the side as if half pitying, half assessing me. "I hope you weren't too bored. I feel like I've been neglecting you. But with rehearsals for the school show and everything else...you know...Lachlan..."

I smirked.

I knew that Liv felt sorry for me. Callum was gone, and for all she knew, he'd simply left me brokenhearted to fend for myself.

Her weekends were filled with rehearsals and time spent trying to convince Lachlan that he was, in fact, her boyfriend. And as far as she was concerned, I had no one.

If only you knew, I thought with the slightest grin teasing the corners of my lips. *If you only knew that I spent this past weekend riding a dragon's back in the Otherwhere, when I wasn't hanging around with my wizard grandfather, my Healer friend or lying in bed with my incredible boyfriend-slash-fiancé...*

I'd treated myself to two nights at the Academy this time, and Callum and I had spent much of the weekend on Caffall's back,

73

looking for evidence of troop movements. We'd watched the queen's Waergs herding Ursals, the oversized, feral bears who inhabited the Otherwhere's Southeast, in a futile attempt to render them compliant enough to recruit them into her army.

After determining that we had several months at least before the queen's troops would be prepared for combat, we met with Merriwether to debate the Academy's next move.

Of course, I couldn't tell Liv about any of it. Not the coming war, or my frequent visits to Callum, or my mysterious grandfather.

None of it.

"Vega?" Liv said, pulling me out of my rapidly-moving train of thought. "I asked what you did this weekend? From the looks of it, though, you either deprived yourself of sleep or got chewed on by a mind-eating zombie."

I laughed. "Sorry—I was a million miles away. I...mostly just watched Netflix," I said with a shrug. "That new Romance series about the Earl. Binged the whole thing in a day."

"All of it? Seriously? Oh, man, you need to start getting out," she told me with a sympathetic lowering of her chin. "Find a new guy—one who won't walk out on you. I'd tell you to date Lachlan, but he's sort of taken..."

"I know, I know," I said. "I'm just...not ready to date anyone. I still have feelings for Callum. It's kind of complicated."

Just as I uttered those words, Miranda, the head of the Charmers, walked by.

"More like you're not over getting your ass dumped by the hottest guy ever to walk into this town," she chortled as her two annoying companions giggled in unison behind her. "It's amazing, you know. Callum was so grossed out by you that he dropped out of school and moved far away. That's some serious revulsion."

It was about the hundredth time Miranda had leveled the

same insult in my direction, so I glared at her but kept my verbal barbs to myself.

It was enough to bask in the satisfaction of knowing that Callum and I were more committed to one another than ever— there was no need to waste my breath on a pubescent harpy.

At least, not *all* my breath.

"Actually, he's coming to visit at Christmas," I said in the most calm, mature tone I could muster. "So I guess the revulsion isn't that strong, after all."

"What?" Liv asked with a gasp. "You didn't tell me *that*!"

I shrugged. "You didn't ask."

"He's probably just showing up so he can dump you again," Miranda retorted, but she was obviously flustered.

"Yes, Miranda," I said. "He's traveling all this way just to dump me, because I'm so despicable. You nailed it, you bloviating she-goblin."

"I don't know what bloviating means, but I'm assuming it has something to do with how bad you smell," she said with a toss of her hair.

"What are you?" Liv asked her, laughing. "Three? It's pathetic —you're so jealous of Vega that the best you can come up with is *you smell like a pile of rancid ferret entrails?*"

"She wasn't quite that graphic, Liv," I protested. "She's not exactly the epitome of wit."

As I was speaking, Lachlan approached us and pressed his back to the locker next to mine, turning to the Charmers and crossing his arms over his chest. "What's going on here?" he asked.

"Oh, the usual," I told him. "Miranda can't resist stopping by to let me know how much I suck. A typical day at Plymouth High."

"Honestly, I don't see why you hang around with these two, Lachlan," Miranda cooed, her tone changing to something high-pitched and saccharine as she looked him up and down. "You're way too good-looking to be friends with the loser crowd."

Lachlan narrowed his eyes and an ominous, threatening growl rose up in his throat. At first, the three Charmers looked as though they thought he was in on Miranda's joke, but after only a few seconds, they turned to storm away in what looked like the coordinated evasive maneuver of a flock of terrified birds.

"What the hell was that?" Liv asked Lachlan with a laugh.

"What was what?" he replied.

"That noise you made. It sounded like some kind of animal."

"Well, I have been called a wild man before," Lachlan said, issuing one of his charming smiles and throwing her a wink.

"Impressive," Liv told him, taking his arm and leading him down the hall toward the stairwell. She turned back and called out, "You'd better tell me about those top-secret Christmas plans of yours at lunch, Vega!"

"Will do!" I yelled back.

Minus the most secret parts.

AT LUNCH, I sat with Lachlan and Liv as usual. To my relief, rather than ask me about Callum's Christmas visit, Liv immediately began to fill us both in about a quick trip her family had taken to Salem on the weekend to visit the House of the Seven Gables, a famous seventeenth-century mansion that many associated with witchcraft.

She pulled her phone out to show us a series of photos she'd taken during their tour. "This is the exterior," she said, flipping through pictures of the dark brown, imposing structure, which reminded me of some of the houses I'd seen in the Otherwhere's towns. Solid, well-built, and ancient-looking, it exuded a sort of magic that couldn't entirely be described with words.

When she'd scrolled through a bunch of photos of various

rooms inside the house, Liv said, "This is me in the secret passageway," showing us a photo of her with her arms in the air, standing in a narrow, bricked-in stairway with an enormous smile on her lips. "It's so cool! It leads to a hidden room and everything."

"Mmm-hmm," I replied, shooting Lachlan a sideways glance.

Secret passageways are all well and good, but when you've seen everything we've seen...

"This is a little café where we had lunch," Liv continued. "It was delicious. I had a tuna melt with the most amazing shake…"

I glanced at the photo, then found myself doing a double take just as she moved onto the next one.

"Wait—could you go back for a minute?"

"Sure…but why are you more interested in a café than in…"

"Just humor me, okay?"

Liv flicked back to the previous photo, and as I leaned in to stare at it, I could feel Lachlan's intense eyes watching me, curious to know what was so engrossing.

"What is it, Vega?" he asked softly.

"It's nothing." I pushed myself to my feet and blurted out, "You know what, guys? Suddenly I'm feeling kind of sick. I think I'll go home for the rest of the day. Great photos, Liv. I'll have to see the rest some other time."

"Wait, what? Why?" Liv asked, staring down at her phone then at me. "Is it something I said?"

"Not at all," I replied with a tight-lipped smile. I looked at Lachlan for a moment before turning to flee the cafeteria. "I'll be back tomorrow," I said. "Promise."

I raced out of the large room, my heart pounding so fast that I struggled to breathe.

For the first time in my life, I was about to cut class.

SALEM

THE PHOTO on Liv's phone had been unremarkable, really. Just a pleasant family portrait like so many others, it showed Liv and her parents, standing in front of a café on a sunny, chilly day.

But it was the sign on the shop next door to the café that had caught my eye:

Suspiria's Collectibles

It was entirely possible that the shop had nothing to do with the Suspiria Solara had told me about in the Otherwhere.

A coincidence?

Maybe.

But I needed to know for sure.

Besides, Mareya had told me I should look for Suspiria in what she called the "Witch Town." I'd foolishly assumed she was talking about some place in the Otherwhere, but now, it was beginning to make perfect sense. What town was witchier than Salem, Massachusetts, famous for its Witch trials in the seventeenth century?

The second I was clear of the cafeteria, I rushed to the stairwell at the end of the hall and tucked myself into a dark corner under the stairs. As quickly as I could, I summoned a small door to bring me to my house, slamming it as I stepped through.

I could have opened another Breach to take me to Salem, straight onto the street in front of the shop. But if this Suspiria was the one Mareya had mentioned—if she *was* actually a proper Witch—I didn't want to give away my nature too soon and scare her off. Conjuring a spell to take me to her would put her on high alert. She could disappear on me, and then I'd never get the answers I was seeking.

Not to mention that I needed time to think, and a drive on a bright, crisp day would give me just that.

I just hoped I was doing the right thing.

THE RUST-MOBILE—THE name I'd given the old Toyota that normally sat dormant in the driveway—protested a little when I tried to coax it to life, sputtering and hacking until it finally began to purr like a contented cat.

The drive to Salem was quiet. The perpetual rush hour that seemed to plague the highways and roads around Boston didn't seem too awful for once, and I was grateful for it as I skirted my way northeast toward the coast.

Even so, it was two hours before I reached the outskirts of Salem.

I'd always had a love-hate relationship with the quirky tourist-attracting town, with its sordid history of the persecution of women combined with an absolute obsession with Witches themselves—there was almost a reverence for the very women the city had once hunted and murdered. The police cars' doors were even emblazoned with the silhouette of a Witch flying on a broom.

Real Witches would have burned the city down long ago, I

muttered under my breath as I drove along Essex Street toward the café where Liv's family had eaten lunch a day earlier.

I pulled into a parking spot a few doors down from Suspiria's Collectibles, slipped out of the car, and proceeded, my heart hammering, toward the shop's door.

In the front window display was an assortment of Witch-related items: wrinkled, green-faced dolls riding brooms. "Healing Crystals" of varying colors and sizes. Vials of what was doubtless tinted water meant to look like actual potion.

I pushed the door open and stepped inside, only to see a young woman with black hair, a streak of purple on one side, working behind the cash register. She shot me a surly glare before forcing a closed-lipped smile and asking what she could do to help.

"I'm looking for the shop's owner, actually," I said.

"The owner?"

"Yes. Suspiria *is* her name, right?"

"Yes, but she doesn't…"

"It's all right, Angelica," a voice called out from somewhere at the back of the store. I turned to see a woman pushing her way through a double-layer of beaded curtains that appeared to lead to a back room. "I'd be happy to speak to our visitor."

The young woman called Angelica clammed up immediately, her expression confused and perturbed at once.

"What can I do for you?" Suspiria asked.

I studied her quickly. Dark eyes, high cheekbones, an impressively sharp nose.

But her most striking feature was a deep scar on the left side of her face. Three parallel scars, really—slash marks that looked as if they'd been left many years ago by a large animal. They didn't detract from her beauty, but they were definitely hard to ignore.

I shot Angelica a look before taking a step forward and asking

Suspiria under my breath, "Have you ever met a woman called Solara?"

Instantly, the color drained from Suspiria's face. Her eyes shifted to her employee, who was busying herself tidying items on a shelf behind the counter.

Suspiria grabbed my arm and pulled me close.

"Come with me," she said, her voice tightly strained.

She led me through the beaded curtains into a back office, where I assumed she would sit me down. But instead, she thrust a hand, palm forward, toward the back wall, which dissolved to reveal an open entryway into yet another room.

Now this *is a secret room*, I thought with a shallow smile. Definitely a little more striking than the brick-lined hidden stairway at the House of the Seven Gables.

"Follow me, please," Suspiria said, guiding me through the opening into the other room, which was windowless but brightened when a series of lights flickered to life along the ceiling.

When the wall had sealed up behind us, Suspiria turned to face me.

"You are a Seeker," she said. "But you are more than that—you have the makings of a Sorceress. I never thought I'd see one of your kind in my lifetime. Certainly not here."

"It doesn't matter what I am," I told her. "I'm not here in the capacity of a Seeker, a Sorceress, or anything but myself."

"You sought me out, and somehow you found me. But your hunt doesn't end with me, does it?"

"It depends on whether you're willing to help me or not," I said, awkwardly tucking a dark curl behind my ear.

On almost every level, Suspiria reminded me of Solara. She was unreadable, distant, beautiful and appraising, all at once.

But she was also more nervous than Solara, as if my finding her was a threat to her very existence.

"You came to ask about the boy," she said quietly, as if afraid someone had their ear pressed to the wall. "The...child."

So, she spoke of him like he was still young. But *how* young?

"Yes," I said. "I want—need—to know where he is."

"Ah. And here I assumed you'd want to know *when* he is." Suspiria turned away from me and walked toward a painting that hung on the far wall. As she moved, a sconce hanging to her left pulled itself away from the wall and followed her, illuminating the portrait of a dark-haired woman walking through what looked like a glowing, round portal.

"Solara chose me to take her sister's son from her," she said, "not because she knew me well, but because I am what's called a Time Leaper. Do you know what that is?"

"I do," I replied. "They're people who can jump through time and back again. Very rare."

And quite dangerous.

"That's right. I chose, with the boy, to jump from the Other-where into this world...to move ahead in time, and never to return."

"Why did you stay here?"

"For one thing, the place suited me. For another, returning would have made it easier for...him...to find me. And that would have put the boy at risk."

Him.

There was no doubt in my mind that she was talking about Meligant.

"When was that?" I asked.

"The exact date escapes me. I did my best not to register it in my mind, in case anyone should ever come inquiring. But we came through somewhere in the vicinity of seventeen years ago."

I tightened. Seventeen years? That could mean that some-where in Salem was a boy around my age. Meligant's son. A chal-lenger for the throne of the Otherwhere.

"Does he...do you..." I began, but Suspiria shook her head.

"Live together? No. Solara wanted him far from Witches. Far from the likes of herself or me, in the hopes that he would remain as human as possible for as long as possible. So I gave him to a young couple who were unable to have children. They were grateful for the gift. They promised to raise him as their own."

"I see. Did you keep in touch with them?"

"No...I..." She paused for a moment, seemingly contemplating her next words carefully. "We have never spoken since that day."

"Where do they live?" I asked, frightened of what the answer might be.

"I wish I could tell you. They used to live in Parkston. They came to Salem to meet the boy and take him home, but at the time, they were on the verge of moving to a new town. I couldn't tell you where, though. I asked them to keep the information from me, for the boy's sake."

"What was their name? Maybe I could find them..."

"Grayson," Suspiria offered with a hard breath. "But Seeker, I am not sure you really *want* to find them."

"Why not?"

She locked her eyes on mine and took a step toward me. "Because for the short time that I had the boy in my possession, I could feel a strength in him. He was powerful, though he was too young to know it—and he may *never* know it. I can only hope he grew up without encountering any users of the High Magic. Because when that boy comes into adulthood, into his own..."

"What?" I asked, holding my breath. "What will happen?"

"His true power will begin to develop, and if he is influenced by the wrong forces, it's entirely possible that he will follow in their footsteps."

"The wrong forces?" I asked.

"His father." Suspiria picked up a dagger that was sitting on a nearby desk, pressing the sharp tip into her finger. "The boy is dangerous. He could destroy you, those you love, and all that you've worked for since your seventeenth birthday. He could destroy us all."

HOME AGAIN

Suspiria was probably right about the child.

Any son of Meligant—of that terrifying man whose eyes I'd looked into—was no doubt dangerous.

Or, at the very least, powerful.

Even if he didn't know it.

Still, something was drawing me to him...or at least to the discovery of his identity. I felt compelled to learn who he was before the truth came at me like a freight train. There was already too much at risk—the Usurper Queen amassing her forces in the Otherwhere. Callum's and the Academy's preparations for the coming war. The missing Orb of Kilarin.

"Thank you," I told Suspiria. "You've been very helpful."

She nodded once and said, "I hope, for your sake, that the boy stays hidden. I hope he never finds out who or what he is, and that he has been raised to value this world. Because if he's capable of half the cruelty of his father..."

"You know Meligant personally?" I asked.

"I know about him," she replied. "I know what he's capable of. The man, unlike his brother, is a creature of pure ambition. He's conniving, manipulative, and any humanity he ever possessed was trampled by his greed. When they were Severed, his dragon —Mardochaios is his name—lost his sight. It was Meligant's doing; a tactic to render the beast reliant on him."

"That's horrible," I said. "I saw that he was blind, but I didn't know it was a deliberate act."

"The dragon is nothing more to Meligant than a weapon of war. They are separated, but the bastard made sure that the beast has no agency. He latches onto the dragon's mind as one would use a grappling hook on flesh—digging in, penetrating, torturing. He is a cruel, empty shell of a man. Let's hope his child doesn't turn out the same."

"The child may take after his mother," I said. "If Tarrah was anything like Solara, her son could turn out to be kind…"

"Let us hope for kindness, then. Because the alternative is too frightening to fathom."

WHEN I LEFT Suspiria's store, I drove back to Fairhaven, more determined than ever to find Meligant's son, despite her warning. If I knew where he was—if I could keep an eye on him—then maybe I could protect him from his father.

But once I'd seated myself in front of my computer, I found myself suddenly sapped of energy. All too quickly, I was learning just what a common name *Grayson* was.

There had to be hundreds in New England alone. And it was entirely possible that the couple no longer lived in the area. They could have moved to Asia by now, for all I knew.

There were no old articles about couples adopting babies. No evidence, no anything.

I shut my laptop and lay down on my bed, staring at the ceiling.

"Where are you?" I whispered, contemplating what a son of Solara's sister and Meligant might look like. I imagined dark hair, intense eyes, high cheekbones. He was probably handsome, whoever he was—not that the theory helped me in the least.

As I lay there uselessly, the doorbell rang once, then again, as if the visitor knew without a doubt that I was home. I pushed myself out of bed and trotted downstairs to answer it, only to see Lachlan standing in front of me, a look of concern in his eyes.

"Vega!" he said. "You feeling better?"

"Better?"

"Um, yeah? Remember several hours ago when you left school because you were feeling sick?"

"Oh—that," I said, forcing out a fake cough. "Yeah, I'm definitely coming down with something."

"You're definitely lying."

"Fine." I frowned, gestured to him to come in, and led him to the kitchen. "I'm lying."

"So what the hell have you been doing all day, then?"

"Trying to solve a mystery that's apparently unsolvable," I lamented. "Which seems futile, I know."

"So maybe it's meant to remain a mystery?" he asked, reaching for the cookie jar on the counter.

"Maybe," I said with a sigh. "Anyhow, whatever. I'm done with it for now."

"Good." We eyed each other for a moment before Lachlan added, "You know, I really miss hanging out with you."

I winced slightly and bit my lip. *Damn it, Lachlan, don't start on your declarations of profound, passionate feelings for me. I really can't take it right now.*

"Sorry," he said, holding up his hands. "Shouldn't have gone there. I didn't mean anything non-platonic by it. I just miss my friend."

With the f-word, a sense of relief washed over me. "It's fine. I kind of miss hanging out with you, too. Though I don't miss watching you almost get killed on my account, or running for our lives when evil assassins come hunting us, or..."

Lachlan popped a small chocolate chip cookie in his mouth, shrugged, and said, "I don't know—I thought those things were sort of fun."

"You're so full of crap."

"A little bit, maybe."

We had a laugh before he asked, "Are you seeing a lot of Callum these days?"

"I am," I replied, evading his gaze. "At least, on weekends. I'm still trying to keep focused on school when I can."

"Ah. Right."

"He's been filling me in," I blurted out, trying to avoid getting into talk of intimacy or Callum's and my not-quite-written-in-stone plans for the future. "On what's happening in the Otherwhere. There are rumblings of the queen's activities, of course. Worries that the war could come sooner than expected. But Callum's doing well, in spite of all of it. Honestly he's like a whole new person since he and Caffall were separated. He seems to be able to breathe now, in ways he couldn't before...if that makes sense."

"Good, I think. Whatever makes him more human."

I narrowed my eyes in an attempt to figure out if he was being sarcastic, and determined that he wasn't. "What do you mean?"

"Nothing, really. I just...sort of envy him sometimes for what he is now. I told you on Thanksgiving that lately, I feel like something inside is eating away at me. Like my wolf—or something entirely different—is uneasy. Unsatisfied. I don't quite know how to describe it. I can only imagine how Callum felt all those years, with a restless dragon inside him. It must be a relief to have been Severed, though I'm sure he misses Caffall at times."

"It was hard for him to coexist with Caffall, actually," I said. "Exhausting, especially toward the end. Caffall didn't like being kept prisoner, and I could see the power struggle hurting Callum each day that they battled each other."

"Power," Lachlan said. "Yeah, that's one word for it."

I stared at him for a moment before asking, "When did you first know?"

"Know what?"

"That you were a Waerg. A wolf shifter."

He contemplated the question for a time before replying, "I'm not sure I can answer that. I don't remember—but that's probably because I was brought into Maddox's pack early on. After that, I was surrounded by Waergs. I suppose it's like being the child of school teachers—you just figure one day you'll become a teacher, too. I just sort of…became a Waerg, I guess. It was like I didn't have a choice in the matter, because that was how my fate steered me."

At that, my brow furrowed. "You can't just *become* a shifter. It's not like I would've become one if I'd lived among the pack like you did."

"I don't know about that," Lachlan laughed. "You're pretty impressive. Every time I see you, you've got a new trick up your sleeve."

"The day I can turn into an animal is the day pigs fly," I retorted.

"Don't underestimate yourself, Sloane. I suspect you *could* make pigs fly, if you put your mind to it."

"You'd better not put any ideas in my head, or I'll be recruiting an army of flying pork to combat the Usurper Queen."

Lachlan chuckled, shrugged, and said, "Anyhow, I guess shifting is in my blood. Who knows?" He went silent for a moment, his face turning serious. "Sometimes I wish I could just be…normal."

"You'd be bored if you were normal, Lachlan. As it is, you're able to turn into a powerful animal. That's pretty amazing."

"Sure, I guess. I just wish I understood my purpose a little better, you know? It's hard to find your place when you're alone. The pack and I hate each other at this point. To them, I'm nothing more than a traitor. I suppose I just wish I had a plan for my life."

"You and me both," I said with a chuckle. "I still don't know if I'm going to college next year, let alone what I'll do with the rest of my life. I mean, I want to be with Callum, of course. But there's so much more to life than relationships. I want to make sure I contribute something to the world."

I glanced over to see a strange look in Lachlan's eye—one I hadn't seen before. It was like he was pondering something in the distance, something I couldn't see or even imagine.

"What's going through your mind?" I asked.

"I suppose I was just wondering—if I were powerful like Callum has always been—if I were that impressive…"

"Yes?"

"I wonder if you'd feel different about me."

I straightened inadvertently, my jaw clenching. "You think I love Callum because he's the heir to the throne?" I asked, slightly offended.

"Not exactly. But it doesn't hurt, right?"

When I glared at him, he shook his head and snickered. "Forget I said it. It was stupid hypothetical, anyhow."

"Okay, good. I don't want to play *what if*, at least not with my feelings. We've already done that too much. Besides, you already know how I feel about you."

"I know you see me as some kind of brother," he replied. "Which I suppose is better than nothing."

"It's huge, actually," I replied. "You're part of my family, Lachlan. That's permanent. That's forever. And I hope I'm part of yours, too. I care deeply about you. I'd do—*almost*—anything for you."

"Those are nice words, Sloane," he said, turning toward the front hall. He was smiling, but somehow he still looked dejected and confused at the same time. "Listen, I'm going to head out now. I'll see you in class tomorrow? I mean, if you're recovered from whatever brief faux-plague incapacitated you today?"

"Of course," I replied, hating how tense we were leaving things. "Hey, I know it's a little early to ask, but would you come for a late dinner on Christmas Eve, after the tree-lighting downtown? My brother will be here. And Callum, and Liv. It would mean a lot if you'd attend, too."

"Wouldn't miss it."

"Good," I said, escorting him toward the door.

When we'd reached it, he turned to face me.

"Sometimes," he said, his tone far away, his eyes fixed on the far wall, "I feel like there's a part of myself I've never met. Is that weird to say?"

"Sort of. But not really," I assured him. "I told you—every teenager feels lost sometimes. It's our lot in life."

"There must be a full moon coming or something," Lachlan joked, pulling the door open and stepping out onto the porch. The sky had gone dark already, bringing a frigid temperature with it. "I guess I'm just feeling off. G'night, Vega."

"Good night, Lachlan."

When he was gone, I inhaled deeply. Something was troubling him—something he couldn't quite bring himself to talk about.

And I wasn't sure I wanted to pry that deeply into his psyche.

A DATE

As usual, I went to see Callum that Friday after school had ended.

Normally when we met up, we spent quiet nights alone together in the Academy's Rose Wing. Occasionally—if we were feeling particularly sociable—we'd dine with Merriwether, Niala, or a few of the students or faculty.

But on this occasion, Callum immediately swept me up into his arms and told me he'd like to take me flying with Caffall.

"Really?" I laughed. "Right away? What's going on?"

"The golden dragon and I haven't had a good flight in a few days. And I'm feeling like we're overdue." He smiled as he said the words, but I wasn't entirely convinced he was giving me the whole story.

"Why do I get the feeling there's more to this than a simple pleasure flight?" I asked.

Callum paused for a moment before answering.

"You're a perceptive one, Sloane," he finally said, his lips dusting my forehead. His tone had altered, and all joviality was gone. "But then again, you know what's coming."

My heart sank. "War, you mean."

"Eventually, yes. I suppose you don't have to be a Seer to know that. The thing is, when Caffall and I were one entity, it was…simpler. I could control his movements—at least to some extent. I could convey my intentions without so much as forming a conscious thought. But now, I find myself having to relearn how we communicate. He and I need to learn again how to move as one, if we're to be effective weapons against the enemy's forces."

"But you two speak silently. I know you do. Isn't that enough to…"

"We can. But I don't want to have to bark orders at him—not even silent ones. Our minds are bonded, just as they always were, but I need to find a way for him to react to my thoughts instantaneously. I want to feel what he feels. We're close, but we're not quite there yet."

I pondered this for a moment, then said, "You want to be like Meligant."

"Meligant?" he asked, a look of disgust turning his lips down.

"Hear me out. I don't mean it in a bad way—just that if his dragon can't see, it relies entirely on him for direction. He's that dragon's eyes, and in a way, he's its mind, too."

"True. I suppose aspiring to his level of connection is what I'm talking about. The difference is that Caffall can see better than I ever will. I simply want to improve our mutual response time, if that makes sense."

"So you want to head out on a sort of training flight with me?" I asked. "Won't I get in your way? Be a distraction?"

"On the contrary. We could use your help. Besides, Caffall likes you. And I kind of like you too, in case you hadn't noticed."

"Now you're just making me blush."

Callum laughed, headed for the French doors that led out to the Rose Wing's balcony, and let out a long, high-pitched whistle.

Within seconds, I could see the outline of Caffall's majestic golden form soaring toward us, his wings cutting through the air.

I wasn't sure whether it was the whistle or Callum's mind that brought the dragon to us.

Either way, I found myself overjoyed to see him. It was an ironic comfort to have such a vicious-looking beast bring such a feeling of calm with his presence.

When Caffall was close enough for us to look into his enormous eyes, his strange, feral voice vibrated through the air between the three of us. Yet I knew it was inaudible to anyone but Callum and me.

~*Meet me in the eastern courtyard*, he said, his eyes locked on Callum's. *We will proceed from there.*

"We'll be there," I replied out loud.

I summoned a Breach and within ten seconds, we were standing at the courtyard's center, even as Caffall came in for a hard landing several feet away, tucking his massive wings in at his sides.

Climbing up with the help of a series of jagged, step-like scales, we made our way onto his back and he took off again, soaring high into the clouds.

As I pressed close to the dragon's body, I thought of Solara and the other Witches who could walk "on the Wind," as she put it—a form of flight that rendered them lighter than air and hidden from those on the ground far below. The Witches didn't need dragons, brooms, or any other magical form of transportation. They simply defied the rules of physics through some sort of masterful mental power.

Then again, so did I.

I wondered if Wind-Walking was a skill I could one day master.

But for now, I was simply grateful to be on the dragon's back once again. There was no feeling in the world quite as invigorating as pressing one's body toward that of an enormous flying creature capable of taking down entire armies.

We flew for some time before Callum leaned down and whispered something to Caffall in a language I didn't understand. It was the language of a shifter and his beast—magical words that existed only for their ears.

"Hang on, Sloane!" Callum shouted as Caffall banked to the left and shot through the air like a bullet, deftly dodging a flock of what looked like large geese flying in formation. Seconds later, we found ourselves beneath the cloud cover, and I could see rocky terrain below us by the edge of the sea.

"See the boulders below?" Callum asked me.

I nodded. "Yes! What about them?"

"I'm going to ask Caffall to obliterate a few of them. Strategically located ones, marked as members of the queen's forces. All in preparation for our combat maneuvers."

I was skeptical, but reminded myself that I'd seen Caffall shoot missiles before, from the back of his throat. Sharp, piercing projectiles that could take down one tree after the other with surgical precision.

Turning again, Caffall darted toward the water, and, flying just above its surface, opened his mouth wide, smoke billowing from his broad nostrils.

I saw a flash, then another, and another, as the targeted boulders exploded into a million pieces, leaving those around them perfectly intact.

"Impressive," I said when Caffall had once again risen into the sky. "Seems like you two have this communication thing sorted."

"We're getting there," Callum said. "But that was just the beginning."

Caffall picked up his pace once again and flew down toward a field that at first appeared to be littered with row upon row of strangely dressed almost-human looking figures.

I quickly realized many of them were mannequins dressed as soldiers—a complicated, detailed mockup of the enemy's forces.

Others wore the colors of the Academy—red, blue, green and silver—and the sigil of the Sword of Viviane.

"This one is a test for us both," Callum said.

"Good luck," I said, tightening with excitement.

Without speaking, Callum managed to guide Caffall low over the figures, and with calculated, fiery breaths, the dragon took out only the ones dressed in the enemy's gear.

Once again, he left all the others untouched.

"How are you two doing that?" I asked Callum. "You didn't even say anything."

"I did," he replied. "Just not with words."

Caffall soared over a broad hill, only to reveal another field. This one was filled with stationary figures who looked more like animals: Grells, Waergs, Aegis cats, and some relatively innocent-looking deer, wolves, foxes, and other creatures.

"Your turn," Callum said.

"My turn?" I asked, twisting around to look at him. "To do what?"

"To guide our living weapon of war."

"But I can't. I'm not…" I was about to say *you,* but realized Callum would never accept that as an excuse.

"In times of battle, I won't always be on his back. You're one of the few people in the Otherwhere who's communicated mentally with dragons—not just Caffall, but five others. It would help me to know you feel comfortable issuing commands."

I tensed again, and Callum laughed. "It's okay. He won't be offended, I promise."

~What is your wish, Seeker? Caffall's voice rang in my mind. *Tell me.*

"They're fake, right?" I asked. "All the creatures down there—they're not real. No adorable bunnies will be harmed in the making of this slaughter?"

"Correct. They were, all of them, conjured for this very purpose."

"Conjured? You mean by a Summoner?"

"Lord Merriwether—your grandfather—cast the spell, though

I don't believe he'd call himself a Summoner, exactly. He has some skills that most of us have never seen."

I laughed. Finally, I was seeing some of my grandfather's handiwork. Impressive.

We circled above the expansive field and I eyed the troops below us, mentally determining where our enemies and allies were in relation to one another.

Caffall, I said silently, *Take out the Waergs.*

~All of them? he asked. *Are you certain?*

I was surprised at the question until I looked again, only to see one Waerg who looked familiar.

He was dark gray and sleek. And on his back, so small that I hadn't even noticed it, was a small pack with the Academy's sigil emblazoned on its side.

"Lachlan?" I said out loud.

A trick. It had to be.

Merriwether wasn't just testing Callum or Caffall—he was testing me, too.

Good eye, I told the dragon. *Don't hurt the one with the sigil.*

~As you wish.

I watched, pressed against Caffall's neck, as the scene below us brightened to a clarity my eyes had rarely experienced. It was like I could see every individual hair, every blade of grass below the enemies' feet. The dragon shot at one summoned Waerg after the other, obliterating them where they stood until all that was left was a field of mostly peaceful looking creatures and the one lone wolf, the sigil adorning his back.

"Well done," Callum said. "That was very skillful of you both."

"I didn't do anything. It was all Caffall."

"You're wrong about that. He was following your thoughts. Your eyes, your mind. You may not have been conscious of it, but where you looked, he went. You steered him without so much as a word—not to take credit from him, of course.

~Thank you, Caffall's voice barreled. *Lord Callum is right. When*

we bond—when we are linked as we were just now—our vision becomes connected. You may have experienced a change in your perception?

"Everything looked ultra-clear to me," I said. "Is that why?"

~It is.

"Amazing."

For the first time, I'd gotten a tiny taste of what it was to be a shifter—to see the world through the eyes of a wild creature, and not just one's own insufficient human ones.

It was incredible.

"Caffall," Callum said, "Vega and I have a few drills of our own to practice. Are you willing to set us down, away from the throngs of fake creatures down there?"

~Of course.

When we'd landed, Callum turned my way.

"All right, Sloane. Now comes the real test."

"I feel like I'm back at the Academy," I said. "You're about to make me do something I really don't want to do…aren't you?"

"Never." Callum winked. "Well, maybe. Could you summon me a sword?"

"Of course." I closed my eyes and pictured an elegant, light-weight blade with a silver and black hilt. After a moment, I felt its weight in my hand and looked at it, smiling as I handed it over.

"I meant for you to summon it into my hand."

"Right," I stammered. "I can do that, too."

I closed my eyes again and called the same sword to appear in Callum's fist.

"Very good," he said. As I watched, he swung the sword around with his usual agility. "Now, I just need a target."

"What sort?" I asked.

"I suppose it would be morbid to ask for a dummy with my sister's face."

"A little…"

"How about a simple scarecrow? Faceless, heartless, brainless."

"I can do that."

When I'd summoned the scarecrow, I stood back and crossed my arms, expecting to watch.

"There's just one more little thing," Callum said, holding the sword up and staring at me.

"Okay," I replied slowly.

"I told you a while back that I'd been having visions of fire and flame."

"You did."

"I've realized something. The flame wasn't coming from me. It was coming from you."

FIRE AND FAILURE

"WHAT ARE YOU SAYING?" I asked Callum, my brow creased with confusion.

"I thought I was having visions of myself conjuring fire," he said. "I thought maybe Caffall's power had rubbed off on me, somehow. That I'd inherited a certain sort of elemental magic because of his ability to breathe fire."

"Okay, so go ahead. Use it," I said, gesturing toward the very innocent-looking scarecrow who was about to burn.

But Callum shook his head. "I had another vision last night. More like a dream, really. I was standing at the head of an army, with the forces of the enemy laid out before me. In my hand was a sword, and its blade was swirling with orange flames. I could feel its power—the strength of the conflagration. It was more than just fire, Vega. It was *magic*. A weapon powerful enough to cut down hundreds of enemies."

"You said it was only a dream," I told him. "Nothing more."

"I'm saying that in the dream, when I turned to look to my left, *you* were standing next to me. And in your eyes, I could see the fire, dancing on your irises. I may have brought the strength…but you were the one who brought the flame. It was *your* magic. You had become a Sorceress of Fire."

"That's a nice fantasy, but…" I shook my head. "I've never cast a spell like that. I'm not…"

"You're not what?"

"I mean, I know that skilled Witches can control the elements. They have specialties, some of them. Fire, Air, Water, Earth. Solara can move through the air like she's walking on the ground. But I'm not Solara. No matter what anyone says, I'm no Witch. I'm a Seeker with a few cool little spells up her sleeve. You've seen me in combat, Callum. I'm useless. It's why you and Lachlan and others are always having to fight for me. I'd be dead if it weren't for people stronger than me."

Still, I stared at the sword for a moment, tempted by Callum's faith in me. Would it really hurt to just *try* it?

"I'm not going to pressure you into anything you don't want to do," Callum said. "But if you'd like to try, now is as good a time as any."

"I'll try. But I can't promise anything."

"That's fair."

I closed my eyes and pictured fire. At first, a mere candle, its small flame flickering weakly. Then a hearth filled with embers, which exploded into a series of dancing flames, growing higher, broader, hotter.

My mind moved to focus on the sword in Callum's hand.

I pictured its silver blade, its elegant hilt.

It was then that my mind failed me.

I couldn't fathom the blade on fire. I couldn't see what Callum had seen.

All I saw in my mind's eye was a silver sword. Simple, elegant, gleaming in the sunlight.

I opened my eyes and shrugged apologetically.

"Maybe it's because you're holding the sword in your hands," I explained to Callum. "I might be subconsciously afraid of burning you."

He stepped forward and stabbed the sword into the scarecrow's torso, backing away. "Try again," he said softly.

I shut my eyes a second time, and invested every ounce of mental strength I had in the task. I thought of Solara, of her ability to harness the Wind, to make herself weightless.

I thought of the Usurper Queen, of how badly I wanted to defeat her armies.

But nothing worked. There was to be no fire.

At least, no fire conjured by my weak mind.

"I'm sorry," I finally said. "I don't think I can. I'm not strong enough."

"It's all right," Callum said, stepping toward me, smiling, and tucking his finger under my chin. "Like I said, no pressure. It's possible that my dreams really were just dreams. Maybe it was all a metaphor for how much I love you. The burning, torturous passion that is adoration, or something."

The left corner of my lip pulled into an off-kilter smile. "I like that metaphor," I said.

He let out a deep-chested laugh and wrapped his arms around me.

"Come on. Let's head back to the Academy, get something to eat, and sit by the fireplace. That's all the heat we need for the time being."

I breathed a deep sigh of relief into his chest.

"That sounds perfect."

AN HOUR LATER, after saying goodbye to Caffall, we were sipping hot chocolate in front of the massive fireplace in our suite's living room.

The carpet we were sitting on was thick and luxurious, and I felt blissfully fortunate to be sharing such an idyllic moment with Callum.

"So," he said after a sip of his cocoa, "the big meeting is coming soon."

"Between you and Will, you mean?"

"That's exactly what I mean."

I put my cup down, pressed my hands into the carpet behind me, and found myself wiggling my toes nervously in front of the fire.

"What are we going to tell him, Vega?" Callum asked softly, reaching out to take a dark curl between his fingers. He edged closer to me—close enough that I could feel his warm breath stroking my neck.

"Tell him?"

"About the future. If you decide—eventually—to live here, he'll need to hear it from you. Otherwise he'll conclude that I'm stealing you away from your world. Neither he nor I could live with ourselves if we thought that was the truth."

"Right. But that's down the road. We don't have to overwhelm him this time around. This is just an initial meeting, really." All of a sudden, I was talking so fast I wasn't sure Callum even understood what I was saying.

He pulled away. I felt his eyes on me for what felt like minutes before I finally dared a glance at him.

"You're avoiding the topic," he said. "Our future…it scares you for some reason. Tell me why."

"Of course it doesn't scare me," I lied, my eyes avoiding his once again.

"Come on. You're sensible—well, usually. You'd be crazy not to let the idea of a lifelong commitment frighten you a little, Vega."

I chewed on my lip, pondering my reply. I had to be honest.

He deserved that much, after all we'd been through together. "It's not the idea of a future with you that frightens me, Callum. I'd spend hundreds of years by your side, if they were guaranteed. If the future were certain—if I could feel confident…"

"You're not confident? Are you worried that I don't love you?"

"Of course not." Wincing a distant pain away, I stared into the flame, searching for the words I needed.

"Then what?"

"I love you," I told him, my voice breaking at last. "More than anything in the world. But I nearly lost you, and it scared me half to death."

"I see."

I choked back a sob as I continued.

"All I can think about is what happens if I let myself—*truly* let myself—be happy, and I lose you all over again? There's a war coming, Callum. And you'll be on the front lines. What do I do, when all this is over, if you…if you die? What do I do if I end up alone, after giving everything up?"

I'd finally said the words out loud—a revelation of fears I'd never even confessed to myself.

The thought of losing yet another person I loved was a constant, chronic terror. And not a day passed when its symptoms didn't paralyze me in some way.

"You haven't lost me," he said. "I'm very much alive, thanks to you."

"I know, I know." I turned his way, tears threatening to stream down my cheeks. "And when it happened, I told myself I was strong enough to deal with anything that came my way. That no matter what happened, I'd be okay. But this awful feeling creeps in sometimes. It holds me back, like I'm tied to a life that's safe, rather than one that's happy."

I took a deep breath and wiped a tear away before continuing.

"When I was a little girl, I thought I could conquer the world.

I was confident, fearless. Then the day came...that horrible day, when Will and I lost our parents. I survived it. But since then, there has always been an ache inside me, so deep, so painful, like a permanent knot of emptiness and pain. The day I met you, that wound began to heal, and I felt myself regaining some of the strength I'd lost. You make my feel whole again. And when I think of you...I feel so strong. It's like I've finally recovered. But the fear of relapse is like a weight around my neck."

Callum stroked my cheek. He was looking at me, listening, his arctic blue eyes piercing into my own. He didn't try to protest, to sway me one way or the other. He was simply present, attentive.

He was perfect.

"When I think about life without you...I know rationally that I'd survive. But it's like..." I bit my lip to keep it from quivering. "It's like the Chasm. Like some part of me would be wounded deeply, forever, and never heal. So instead of taking the risk, I find myself putting up a shield. Telling myself to hesitate, to hold back, to commit to nothing instead of everything. Just in case the blade is about to slice into me."

He took my hand, brought it to his lips, and held onto it as he spoke.

"I can't promise I'll never die," he said. "But you have to decide if you want to spend your life living in fear of losing me, or if you can accept being with me until the day when one of us is no longer here. I've told you before, I'm not going to pressure you into something that makes you unhappy. I love you too much to want to shackle you to a life of misery."

The truth was that Callum would most likely outlive me by centuries. I was still, for all intents and purposes, mortal. I'd seen myself age and change over the last months, while he'd remained the same strong, extraordinary young man I'd met in July.

I wasn't like Callum.

I never would be.

But that didn't mean I had to live in fear that my life would one day crumble.

"I can't imagine being with you and being unhappy," I admitted. "Besides, I'd rather be happy for a few short months than never."

"Then be happy," he said, lying back, one arm behind his head. "I am yours, Vega Sloane. Forever, if you'll have me. I'll spend my life trying to ensure that each morning, you wake up with a smile on your face. But I can't promise you perfection. No one can."

"Ugh," I said, pulling myself down to kiss him. "Why do you always have to be so rational?"

"Simple. Because I know exactly what I want," he said. "By the way, I have something for you…if you'll accept it."

I narrowed my eyes at him. "What is it?"

He reached into his pocket, pulled out a small, square box, and handed it to me.

"It's a little more permanent than the last one," he said, "but I don't want it to freak you out. It's merely a symbol, not a demand."

I cracked the box open to see a ring inside.

It was crafted of curving, glistening silver. At its center was an elegantly twisting spiral of metal, and on either side of the spiral was a small, dark red stone.

"Drakestone?" I asked, admiring the ring as I twisted it around, staring at it from every angle.

"It is," Callum replied. "The stone that brought us back to one another—with the help of a certain scepter, of course."

I stroked a fingertip over the two red stones, marveling at their depth, their intensity. Recalling the terrifying moments I'd spent climbing, trying to pry the crimson stone out of the cliff face in the far North in hopes of bringing Callum back to me.

"It's perfect," I said, my eyes welling up.

"May I?" he asked, propping himself up and putting a hand out.

I handed him the ring, which he slipped onto my finger. "Your brother may ask questions," he said. "So I won't be offended if you choose to wear it on the silver chain around your neck."

I smiled. "For tonight, at least, I'll wear it on my finger. Tomorrow, I'll put it on the chain. But I promise you that soon, the day will come when I'll be ready to show it to the whole world."

THE VESSEL

I WAS SITTING in my living room in Fairhaven a few days later when I realized with a shock that Christmas was only a week away.

For all my excitement about the coming holiday, I'd done little to prepare. I'd set up the small artificial tree that sat for most of the year in a corner of the basement, covered in lights and ornaments that my mother had hung when I was a child.

I'd wrapped a few presents for Will, Liv, Callum, and Lachlan, being careful not to spend too much on any of them.

I'd never actually told Will about the massive two-million-dollar deposit our grandfather—a grandfather he didn't even know existed—had made to my bank account months earlier.

Though one day I would have to find a way to tell Will about the money, I'd never quite figured out how I could do so without him deciding to call a team of psychiatrists to come take me away in a truck with a built-in padded cell.

Or he could report me to the authorities for robbing a bank, which would seem like a much saner reaction than believing that a magical wizard from another world had simply dropped a cool two million in my account.

So for now, I had no choice but to maintain the semblance of a starving student living on ramen noodles and stale bread...or whatever scraps of unappealing food starving students were supposed to consume for their meager nourishment.

As excited as I was about the prospect of having Will come to visit, it was knowing he and Callum would soon meet properly for the first time that made my heart feel like it was about to explode with joy.

Something told me they'd get along great—though I wasn't sure how Will would feel if he knew how powerful our feelings were for each other.

Or that I spent each Friday night in Callum's bed...

Will had always been a protective older brother, and explaining the intensity of my bond with Callum without explaining the circumstances that threw us together...was going to be a challenge.

The good news was that it looked like I wouldn't need to learn to harness the elements before Christmas Day. The weather forecasts were calling for heavy snow on the morning of Christmas Eve, continuing for twenty-four hours. That would mean lots of cloud cover for Caffall to conceal himself.

Not that he'd be particularly happy to have to fly around a frigid sky all day and night. I'd have to find a way to thank him one day, though I wasn't quite sure how one properly thanked a dragon. I wasn't about to offer him a goat carcass or sixty pounds of steak.

Maybe a nice, raw, Christmas turkey?

Focus on the people for a minute, Vega, I muttered to myself, going through a mental checklist for the days surrounding the twenty-fifth.

Plans were coming together, but I couldn't help feeling like there was one thing left dangling in the air:

The mystery of Meligant's son.

THE WEDNESDAY AFTERNOON BEFORE CHRISTMAS, I found myself in the midst of some last-minute shopping on Fairhaven's High Street. A mug for Liv's mother. A book for her father.

Toward the end of my errands, I popped into a shop I'd always loved—a sort of combination gift shop and café not far from the Novel Hovel. It smelled of cinnamon, and was filled with the sorts of items one would only ever buy as gifts for other people: expensive, colorful slippers. Mugs with pithy sayings emblazoned on their sides. Playing cards with funny pictures of adorable dogs.

Completely unnecessary but endearing bobbles.

The shop contained the occasional ancient-looking treasure, as well. Slightly-tarnished chalices, mismatched antique silver cutlery, framed bits of stained glass from old, destroyed churches presumably scattered all over the world.

As I wandered the shop, one of the unique items stood out to me: A strange, small ceramic pot with intricate, Celtic-looking details around its perimeter. It was about the size of a sugar bowl, though I couldn't entirely imagine it sitting on anyone's dining table.

What drew me in was its lid, which featured the squat figure of a dragon, curled up as if it was either waiting for something exciting to happen or contemplating a long nap.

I picked the vessel up and stared at it for a moment, turning it around once or twice. As my eyes met the small dragon's face, his own eyes seemed to light up for the briefest moment before fading again.

I glanced around, trying to figure out if anyone else had seen it, but the shopkeeper—a cheerful, bright-eyed woman in her sixties—was busy assisting a customer, and no one else was in the shop.

I popped open the ceramic lid and looked inside, only to see that the vessel was empty. But as I stared into its depths, I was certain that an image was beginning to materialize. I could see…a figure walking toward me through a thick sort of mist…or was it a blizzard?

I couldn't make out any features. Only what seemed to be a man, his face cloaked in shadow.

But then the image faded, and once again the bottom of the small dish was visible.

Though part of me wanted to lay the vessel down and never look at it again, I felt compelled to bring it with me to the counter. Whatever had just happened—whether it was through the vessel's powers or mine—felt important.

There was no way I was leaving the small pot behind.

"A great choice," the shopkeeper said as she slipped behind the counter. "I see you're buying the Graysons' piece."

At hearing that name, I froze and stared at the woman.

"Excuse me—what did you just say?"

"The Graysons' piece," she repeated. "Why? Do you know them? They lived on Ashland, a few blocks away, for years. Such a nice couple. They were—*are*—collectors."

"Collectors? Of what?"

She shrugged. "You name it. Mostly artifacts from various parts of the world. Some of them, like this ceramic jar, are very special. They've always had a penchant for unique items with mythological elements. This one was supposedly used by a Witch in Salem to store herbs of some sort…" She leaned in and whispered the next part. "Though I don't go in for all that witchy nonsense, of course."

"A Witch in Salem," I parroted softly before collecting myself. "You said the Graysons collect items like this?"

"Last I saw them they did, yes. Of course, that was ages ago. I suppose it sort of became an obsession of theirs all those years ago, when their…"

With that, she clammed up and bit her lip, then proceeded to wrap the dragon vessel in layers of tissue paper and insert it into a delicate-looking white paper box.

"When what?" I asked quietly.

The shop owner's eyes met mine, and I focused every ounce of mental energy on holding her stare.

Tell me. I need to know.

I sent the words her way without knowing exactly why I was even doing it. An attempt to coerce, to persuade.

Though it wasn't like it was going to work. I wasn't some kind of mind-controlling wizard.

The shopkeeper leaned toward me and said in a slow drawl, "When they lost their boy."

"Oh," I replied, shocked that she'd been so forthright with me. "That's so awful. They...*lost* him?"

She nodded. "It was the saddest thing. He was only two at the time. I never learned what happened, exactly. They used to come around with him in a stroller, all proud as peacocks. You know the look. Then one day, it was just the two of them again. I'll never forget the moment I first saw them. Their faces had taken on this sort of haunted look, like something terrible had happened—they'd gone pale, and all the life had left their eyes. I never saw the boy with them again. The worst part was that they'd tried for so long to have a child, and finally they adopted him, thinking he was theirs for life. For such a thing to happen..."

"So...he died?"

"That's what people said. Though they never said it in so many words, at least not to me. Come to think of it, I don't recall a funeral. Then again, what sort of a funeral do you have for one so young? It must have been just devastating. They probably kept it private."

"Yes..." I said as I paid for the dragon vessel. "It must have been awful for them." With that, I thanked her and left the shop.

There was no doubt in my mind that the child she was talking about was Meligant's son.

"If he's dead," I said to myself as I walked down the street, "why is Meligant so determined to find him?"

When I'd returned home, I removed the small ceramic vessel from its box, set it on the kitchen island, and stared at it for a few seconds, before lifting it carefully to look at its base.

The words were painted in tiny, faded letters on the flat bottom:

Suspiria's Collectibles
Salem, MA

A NIGHT IN THE ROSE WING

THAT EVENING, I went to visit Callum. I told him nothing of my discovery, of the strange, sad journey I'd been on. All I wanted was to be with him, and to forget about the Graysons and their ill-fated child.

He held me as we lay in bed, and we talked about his coming visit, which managed to cheer me up a little.

"Looking forward to it?" he asked.

"You'll love Will," I promised him for the thousandth time, my head leaning on his chest. "And Liv will be so happy to see you."

"And Lachlan?" he asked. "Do you think he'll be happy that I'm there?"

"He likes you," I said, pulling up to look into his intense blue eyes. "Why wouldn't he be happy to see you?"

Callum's jaw tensed for a moment before he cracked a smile and shook his head. "I don't know why I asked that," he said. "Just a feeling. He sees me as competition, even if he's not entirely conscious of it."

"Competition?"

"For your affection, among other things."

I pondered that for a minute. Lachlan did have a funny habit of comparing himself to Callum—a lot. I'd always attributed it to some male ego thing. It wasn't anything I took particularly seriously. Any young man who had Callum Drake in his sights would probably feel a little insecure around him, after all. Callum was the most impressive person I'd ever met.

"Well," I said, twisting myself around to plant a kiss on his lips, "Just in case, I can assure you there's no reason to be jealous of Lachlan. But come to think of it, jealousy would be sort of cute."

"I'm not jealous," he said, putting his hand around the back of my neck, kissing me hard, then smiling again as he pulled away. "Jealousy is an emotion for people who are insecure—and I am not insecure. At least, not where you're concerned. I've never had so much faith in anything as I do in the certainty that you love me."

As he spoke, he pulled at the chain around my neck, taking the silver ring between his fingers.

"I know," I replied. "I know that *you* know."

"I also know that if ever you decide you'd like to spend your life away from me," he added, "I'd survive. Not happily, of course. But you, Vega Sloane, are a strong, intelligent woman, and I would never want you to stay with the likes of me against your will."

"Well, I'm very grateful to know you don't plan on shackling me in the dungeons in order to secure my hand in marriage, or whatever it is that evil weirdos do in fairytales."

"It I ever shackled you in a dungeon," he laughed, "it would only be for fun."

"I've spent enough time in dungeons for one lifetime, thanks," I chuckled. "There are other, better ways to amuse ourselves."

"Such as?"

"Such as flying around on Caffall's back. Winning a war. Installing you on the throne you deserve."

"And then?"

"And then, living happily ever after...whatever that may mean."

"That *whatever* has a lot of weight to it," Callum said, sitting up, his back straightening. "I know there are many conditions that must be met in order for us to be together in the end. And my Severing from Caffall only made things more complicated. Had I been able to come live in your world..."

I shook my head. "You couldn't have. No matter what. You can't be in my world and rule the Otherwhere. And the Otherwhere needs you. So much has been happening...the queen's armies mobilizing. Meligant coming back after so many years... you're a force for good in this place. You're the leader the Otherwhere needs."

"And you're the woman I need."

At those words, my heart fluttered.

Nothing made me happier than knowing with every cell in my body that he loved me. It was like a warm, enveloping blanket of bliss, a protection against every fear that had ever eaten away at my mind.

Still, I found myself hesitating when I searched my mind for a reply.

"Maybe so," I finally said, "but I'm torn between two worlds. My life is in two parts right now, and I have to figure out how to...be."

Callum leaned back, the sheets falling away from his chest to reveal a body that was powerful, beautiful perfection. I pulled my eyes away, unwilling to get absorbed in the exquisiteness of him while we were having such a heavy conversation.

"Tell me something," he said quietly, reaching over, tucking a finger under my chin and pulling my eyes to his as he so often did. It was a move that made me melt each time—one that reminded me of the moment we'd met in the bookshop in

Fairhaven. The moment when, without fully understanding what was happening, I'd fallen in love with him.

"What do you want to know?" I murmured.

"If your grandparents—if Merriwether and your Nana—could have found a way to stay together without one of their lives being destroyed—do you think they would have done it?"

"In a second," I said without hesitation. "I think they'd even do it now, if they could. Every time they speak of one another, there's so much love, still…after all these years. It's like this energy in the air around each of them. Like it never faded, not even a little bit."

"Well, then. Here is my proposal for you, Vega, my love: If, at the end of all this, we can figure out a way to be together without sacrificing our individual selves, let's try. If we fail, we fail. But losing you because I didn't make every effort to hold onto you is the one regret I don't want to live with for the rest of my life." He swallowed and turned his eyes to the far window, as if he couldn't look at me while he spoke the next words. "I want you to understand that I am freeing you—if freedom is what you decide you want. If you want to stay in your world, or be with someone else…If you feel that life with me means surrendering who you are…"

I pulled back, my jaw tightening. "Who on earth could I possibly want to be with?" I half-laughed. "I love you."

"I know. And I love you. Let's leave it at that for now, okay?"

He pulled me close and kissed me gently at first, but I lay my hands on his stubbled cheeks and pressed my body to his, intent on showing him how much I truly wanted him—how much I would always want him.

We spent the night entwined, and when I finally drifted off, I dreamed of blizzards, mysterious, shadowy men, and a dragon silhouetted against the night sky, flying toward me, a ball of flame forming in the depths of its throat.

As I watched and waited for the searing pain of dragon fire, I felt a layer of armor grow like a second skin over my limbs, my chest, my back.

A moment later, I saw a wall of flame, and then…

Nothingness.

THE GRAYSONS

SITTING in my room the next afternoon, I opened my laptop and looked up the only house in Fairhaven owned by anyone called Grayson.

It seemed the couple had moved from Ashland Street to Parker Avenue several years back. Their new home, more isolated, was situated just on the edge of town, several blocks from where I lived.

Callum would have told me to leave it alone. To let them be, and to forget the child they'd adopted years ago. But I couldn't. As long as dreams of shadowy figures, dragon fire, and death insisted on making their way into my sleep at night, I would be haunted by a mysterious unknown.

I needed to find out what happened to the boy. I had to know for sure that he was no longer in danger.

If only for Solara's sake.

I threw on my winter coat and boots and began the walk over to Parker Street, carefully pondering what I'd say if anyone actually opened the door. But there was little I could come up with that didn't sound downright awful.

What words could I possibly utter that wouldn't sound completely off the rails?

"Hi, my name's Vega, and I'm here to ask about your dead son."

"Hi, could you tell me if your child really died, or was his death something you faked for some nefarious purpose?"

"Hi, I'm a horrible person about to ask you really cruel questions. May I come in?"

It wasn't exactly an easy topic to bring up.

After fifteen minutes or so I found myself standing on the sidewalk, eyeing the Graysons' home. The house was set back from the street, tucked behind a tall row of overgrown hedges that looked almost as though they'd been allowed to run wild in order to keep people away.

I made my way up the weed-covered path to the front steps, and when I'd trudged up to the steps to the front porch, I took a deep breath, told myself everything would be fine, and knocked.

After thirty seconds or so, the door creaked open, revealing a man who looked to be in his late fifties. He was tall, with dark, thick eyebrows, graying hair, and eyes that could only be described as kind, but sad.

"Yes?" he said, his voice hoarse.

"Hi—um—I'm very sorry to intrude, but I'm looking for the Graysons," I told him.

"You've found them," the man said, his eyebrows knitting together as if he could sense that I hadn't come to deliver free girl guide cookies. "What can I do for you?"

"Michael? Who is it?" a woman's voice asked from another room.

"I'm not sure," the man replied.

The woman stepped into the foyer, her eyes going wide when she saw me. She stopped in her tracks, nearly dropping the cup of tea she was holding.

She was wearing a pair of jeans and a comfortable-looking

sweater. She was pretty, with wavy brown hair and a kind face, though her eyes, like her husband's, looked sad in a way that made me wonder just how cruel the world had been to the couple.

Haunted, I thought. *Either by memories, or by a lack of them.*

"My name is Vega Sloane," I said. "I live over on Cardyn Lane..."

"Sloane," the woman said, looking at her husband for a second before adding, "I met your parents a long time ago." She seemed to collect herself, smiled faintly, and said, "Come in. Have a cup of tea. Michael, would you mind shutting the door behind our guest?"

Silently, her husband did as she asked.

"My name is Kathryn. And you've met Michael, of course," my hostess said as I stepped inside, removed my boots and coat, and followed her into the kitchen. She gestured to me to take a seat at a small wooden table as she poured three cups of freshly-brewed peppermint tea.

"You're here because of him," she said, taking a seat opposite me.

I could see her husband, who was standing at her side, open his mouth to speak, but she reached out and squeezed his hand as if to silence him.

"Him?" I asked, unsure why I was pretending not to know who she was talking about.

"The child we looked after for a time," she said, pulling her eyes to the window to watch the large white flakes that had just begun to fall from the sky. "I don't feel worthy to call him our son, you see. We didn't *earn* the title of parents. We...failed him."

"So, you did adopt a boy," I said. "Seventeen years ago."

"Closer to eighteen, actually." Mrs. Grayson eyed her husband, who nodded solemnly. "We...we seldom talk about him," he said. "It's a bit of a sore subject, to put it mildly."

"Of course," I replied, hunting for words, my mind reeling as I felt myself creeping closer to the truth. "To lose him like you did…I can't imagine."

"Lose him?" Mrs. Grayson said. "Oh—of course. I forget sometimes that everyone thinks he died. Back then, it was easier to let them think it. We wanted peace and quiet. We didn't want questions, and nothing makes people more reluctant to ply you with questions than death."

As she spoke, a memory came to me. One time, when Will and I were watching a movie on the couch, I'd expressed how upset I was when a certain character had died.

He shook his head and told me there was no way the man was actually dead.

"How can you say that?" I'd asked. "We saw him fly off a building!"

"Because," he replied, "In movies, if someone's *really* dead… there's always a body."

As I looked at Kathryn, my heart fluttered, and I couldn't entirely tell if I was feeling joy or terror.

My hands trembled under the table as I asked the question.

"So—you're saying he's not dead?"

"Not as far as we know," Michael replied.

"What my husband means is we lost touch after he was taken away," his wife interjected when my expression turned to puzzlement. "For his sake."

"Taken away?" I asked, my eyes moving back and forth between the couple. "I'm confused. Someone took him from you?"

Kathryn let out a sigh. "How much do you know?" she asked. "About the boy—about where he came from?"

"I know a fair amount," I replied, not wanting to divulge too much of the truth about the Otherwhere, or Solara's connection to him. "I know he's…special."

"You know the woman who brought the boy to us was a Witch, then," Kathryn said.

I tensed to hear a human mention Witches as if she believed in their true essence—in their power. But of course she did. The woman in the shop had mentioned that the Graysons had become fascinated with mystical objects. Witches. Magic.

"I do," I replied. "I met Suspiria recently."

"Ah." Kathryn took a sip of tea. "She's a kind woman. What she did—bringing him here, helping him to find a family—that was pure benevolence. It's part of the reason we felt so wretched when we had to give Marcus up."

"Marcus?" I asked.

"That was his name. For a brief time, anyhow, until…until we parted ways. And for the record, it was a difficult choice for us. We struggled with it for months before we decided to give him away. We just…" She looked up at her husband, who laid a hand on her shoulder and offered an affectionate squeeze.

"We couldn't give him what he obviously needed," Michael said.

"I'm sorry," I replied. "I know this must seem awful and strange—me coming here like this and asking these questions. I'm not judging you. I'm only looking for some answers."

"Why?" Michael asked, his tone turning hostile. "Why, after all these years, would a teenage girl be asking about him?"

"Michael," his wife said. "She's not doing any harm."

"She's hurting you," he growled. "Opening up old wounds."

"I'm sorry," I repeated, pushing myself away from the table. "I didn't intend to hurt anyone. It's just…I'm trying to find him. I'm trying to find your son."

THE WOMAN

"I SEE," Kathryn said.

She didn't ask why I wanted to find the child. She winced, like the very thought of seeing him again was frightening to her.

"All those years ago, when Suspiria brought the child here, we were young and naive. She warned us that he wouldn't be like other children. She said we'd not only be protecting him, but ourselves, as well. We wanted a baby so badly that we thought we could overcome any obstacle, and we told her so. But she warned us about what may happen if we took on the...responsibility."

"Warned you?"

"She said the boy came from volatile parents. Difficult ones, with strong temperaments." She smiled for a moment as if recalling some distant memory. "You know, I didn't believe in Witches for most of my life. I thought they were just a fun type of fairy tale character made up to frighten kids. But Suspiria—she had an aura about her. I don't know how to describe it. There was a sort of light around her, and I never could figure out if it was a sign of good or evil. After she left—after what happened with little Marcus—I became fascinated with the idea of Witches.

I've read about them, I've studied them. I've wished I could be one. The power they possess is…"

Her voice trailed off, and her eyes went distant. Once again, I could see her husband squeezing her shoulder, and she crossed her arm over her chest to press her hand to his.

"I see," I said. "Yes—Witches *are* fascinating."

"You said you've met Suspiria. Have you met others?"

"I have," I nodded. "Quite a few."

"Honestly, when I first saw you standing in the doorway, I thought you were one," Kathryn said. "You're lovely, like they are. Your eyes—they feel like they know so much more than you're letting on. There's a glow to you—something intangible. Like I can feel your power on the air."

When I smirked, she let out a strange giggle. "Sorry—I must sound like a lunatic to you, talking about all this."

"Not at all," I said. "I've seen some…interesting things." I sipped my tea before asking, "You said Suspiria warned you about the child. What did she say, exactly?"

"She told us his parents were powerful. That he, too, might turn out to be powerful in ways no one anticipated. But for a time, he seemed so…normal. He was a sweet little thing. For the first year, it seemed like all he did was sleep and laugh."

"And what happened after that?"

"He grew. Little by little, like all babies do. He became more energetic, more demanding. Soon, he was crawling, then walking, then running. I was working full-time—we both were. Like all new parents, we had no idea how to raise a child. But it was when he began to exhibit strange tendencies that I began to doubt our capacity to take care of him."

"What sorts of tendencies?" I asked.

The Graysons threw each other a look. Michael gave Kathryn a nod before she said, "I would walk into his room at night and find him wide awake, silently staring at me. His eyes…they would flash, like the eyes of a cat when a light reflects in them. It frightened me, truth be told. It didn't seem right—even with everything Suspiria had warned us about."

"I see," I said. I'd seen that flash, that reflective quality. In many, many eyes.

"We tried to contact Suspiria, but we couldn't find her anywhere. And as the baby grew a little, he started to show signs that we wouldn't be able to suppress his true nature, no matter how much we might want to."

"Signs?"

Once again, the Graysons exchanged a knowing look. "You'll think we're insane," Michael said.

"Trust me, there's nothing you could say to me that would make me think that," I assured him. "Like I said, I've seen many things."

"One day," Kathryn said, "I went into his bedroom to check on him. But when I walked up to his crib…"

"Yes?"

"There was a creature in there. Snarling, thrashing, baring its fangs at me. It was small, but vicious."

"A creature?" I asked. "What kind?"

"That was the strange thing. To this day, I couldn't tell you. He had fur, and fangs and claws. But he also had wings, like a bat's, or…Anyhow, he wasn't like any creature I'd ever imagined, let alone seen."

"Wings," I muttered, resisting the urge to tell them about Meligant's history. "So, what happened?"

"It took me a minute to realize the creature I was seeing was our child. He finally…changed…into his human form, and I gave him a dose—a sedative the doctor had prescribed. Just enough to send him into a deep sleep. When he woke up, he seemed back to normal."

After another sip of tea, Kathryn added, "We finally heard from Suspiria some weeks later. She came by, just as you did, and asked about the boy. It was like she knew something was happening with us. Like she knew something had changed."

"That's strange," I replied. "She told me she never saw you again, after that first time."

Kathryn frowned. "I don't know why she'd say that. Maybe she forgot. It was a long time ago."

"Maybe," I said.

But something told me she'd deliberately concealed the truth. The question was why?

"Did she take him away herself?" I asked.

Mrs. Grayson shook her head. "*She* didn't take him, no. But she looked him over and told us there was no way to fully suppress what he was…that there was no way to keep his powers entirely contained. The best we could hope for, she said, was to have him live among others who were…*gifted*. Then, his power wouldn't have to be entirely contained, but it could adapt. Her hope was that he would develop to fit into an environment better suited to his needs—that he would become what those around him were. She said he would be safer with a new family, and that we would, too."

"That must have been hard—deciding to let him go."

Kathryn nodded. "It is very painful to lose a child, even if the loss is for the child's own good. But we had no choice anymore. To keep him with us would have been selfish, not to mention dangerous, both for us and him. It would have meant trying to twist him into something he wasn't."

"Human, you mean." I tried my best to utter the word without judgment. "You would have had to try and make him human."

"Yes."

"So, what happened to him? Where did he go?" I asked.

"Suspiria brought a woman to meet us one day. She had dark hair—or was it light? So strange. I can't remember now." Kathryn turned to her husband and asked, "Do you?"

"I really don't," he said.

"You have to understand," Kathryn added, "we were both distraught. I think we both had tears in our eyes the entire time, so details escape us."

"Of course. Do you recall anything else about her?"

"She was elegant, wealthy-looking, well-dressed. Charming, not to mention extremely confident. She was everything we were not. I put the boy into her care, and she promised to raise him as though he were her own. I believed her—we both did. I've never met anyone who seemed so sure of herself."

"The woman—do you remember her name?"

Kathryn bit her lip and frowned. "I don't…though I'm sure it's at the back of my mind somewhere. To be honest, I didn't want to remember it—I didn't want to think about her, or him. The guilt was too much."

"The boy—do you think his last name would still be Grayson?"

"I don't think so. I remember the woman said she would change his name to something no one would recognize—so he wouldn't be traced back to Suspiria or us. She said it was for the best, and we agreed. I'm so sorry—I know you came here for answers, and here I am, with none to give you."

"It's okay," I said. "Thank you for everything you've said. I appreciate it. I know it's hard. Do you know where she is now?"

Kathryn shook her head. "Oh, no. I remember that she said she was considering moving to the area, but I can't say I've ever seen her since that day. Michael and I became reclusive, after…well, we hardly speak to anyone now."

I put my teacup down and rose to my feet. "Thank you both so much for everything. You've been so helpful." I nodded thanks to Michael as well before asking, "Could you do me one favor?"

"Of course," Kathryn said.

"Could we exchange phone numbers? In case you remember anything else—anything that could help me find the boy."

When she nodded, I recited my cell's number for her, and she gave me hers, which I typed into the contact list on my phone.

"Thanks again," I said before making my way to the front hall to put on my coat and boots.

"You never told us why you want to find him," Kathryn said, standing with Michael a few feet away.

I looked at them both, smiled, then said, "Because I want to protect him from someone who might want to hurt him," I said.

"Protect him? But you're just..." Michael began, but he stopped himself.

I knew what he was going to say. You're just a girl. What can you possibly do against whatever beast his father is?

I smiled again.

"You might be right, Mr. Grayson," I said. "But something tells me I'm the one who needs to find the boy. And something tells me I'm the *only* one who can help him, when the time comes."

"I hope you're right," Kathryn said.

I left without another word, a strange, quiet fear brewing inside my chest as I walked home, large flakes of snow dancing around me like silent guardians.

I still had no idea who the boy was, let alone where.

All I knew was that the thought of learning the truth filled me with a dread unlike any I'd ever experienced.

CHRISTMAS EVE

THE MORNING of Christmas Eve arrived with the snow Callum had requested...but it was entirely Mother Nature's work, and not mine.

I'd spent some hours with the book Mareya had given me, studying spells and practicing the few that didn't risk causing serious damage to my house.

But summoning entire weather systems was a little beyond my abilities, to put it mildly.

Enthralled by the sight of falling snow, I rose from my bed and stepped toward the window, stretching my arms over my head with a happy groan as I watched a swirl of flakes tumble half-sideways as they made their way toward the ground. They danced a little as they did so, like they were in no rush to meet their destination.

As I watched the fluttering ballet, my phone let out a high-pitched wail from somewhere behind me, and I sprang over to the bedside table to answer it.

"Hello?"

"Vega—it's Will. I'm at the airport. Just calling to say I'm about to get on my flight."

"I'm so happy to hear that!" I replied with a huge grin. "But I hope your plane can land—the weather is pretty terrible at this end of the country."

"It's all good. I'm flying into Boston, and so far, at least, they're saying it's still clear there. I'll take the train to Wind River, and a taxi from there."

"You don't want me to pick you up?" I asked, admittedly somewhat relieved. Wind River was at least half an hour away, and driving in snow terrified me even more than Waerg encounters—which was saying a lot.

It would have been simple enough to open a Breach to Logan airport and bring Will back through to Fairhaven, of course. But explaining it would have been another matter entirely.

"No, it's fine," he said. "I'm more than happy to get there on my own. Besides, the Rust-Mobile would probably die somewhere on the road halfway back to Fairhaven, and quite frankly, that would suck."

"Fair enough. It *does* cough and sputter a lot these days. Can cars catch cold?"

"I really hope not," Will laughed. "Listen, I'm really looking forward to seeing you."

"Me too. And Will...there's someone I want you to meet. Someone special."

"Oh?" Will went silent for a moment. "This someone—is it..." He stopped as a loud announcement rang out over the airport's system. "Damn it, I have to board. I'll see you in a few hours. We're heading to the tree-lighting in the Commons tonight, yeah?"

"Of course. Wouldn't miss it for anything."

The tree-lighting was an annual tradition in which every single inch of above-ground greenery in the Commons, Fairhaven's large downtown park, was lit up with multicolored strings of festive lights. As with every other annual celebration, the entire town came out to witness the event.

The last time Will and I had attended festivities together in the Commons was Midsummer Fest, on my seventeenth birthday. The day I'd met Callum.

The day I'd discovered my powers.

It seemed like years had passed since that night. So strange to think it had only been a few months.

When I'd hung up the phone, I stepped over to the mirror hanging on my wall and assessed myself, wondering if Will would notice a change in me.

My eyes were definitely different. They'd once been a sort of nondescript hazel. Dull and lifeless, or at least I'd always thought so. But now, they ranged anywhere from bright green to amber-colored to a deep gray, depending on my mood and focus.

Right now, they were a sort of light gray-green, in stark contrast to my dark lashes.

My face had thinned out a little, and my cheekbones had grown more pronounced since my birthday.

I looked…mature.

Weird.

I stared at myself, a rare jolt of confidence surging through me as I determined that I could no longer deny a certain prettiness. I wouldn't have gone so far as to call myself beautiful, as Callum so often did. But I wasn't half-bad, really.

More importantly, I felt powerful, like my newly altered face was a reflection of the changes that had occurred inside me over the last few months. My features were a road map of my experiences, my successes.

Even my failures.

The eyes that looked back at me now were those of a person who understood that the world was a complicated place, filled with threats and surprises that lurked around every corner. The girl who stared out at me had been through near-death experiences. Heartbreak. Joy. She'd fallen in love. She'd developed life-long friendships…and made mortal enemies.

She was kind of a mess. But at least she didn't look any the worse for wear.

I didn't have Callum's strength, or Solara's wisdom. But I was learning. I was growing. And one day, I'd come into my own.

As long as I didn't die first.

Shaking my head at myself in reprimand for my seemingly constant string of morbid thoughts, I grabbed my robe and headed to the bathroom to shower.

I had no idea what time Callum would arrive in my world with Caffall. He'd assured me that they would make their way through what he called a *sky-portal*—a Breach that some magic user or other had created some years ago—and that I didn't need to worry about heading to the Academy to get them.

"Merriwether showed it to me long ago," he told me. "It's how I came to Fairhaven the first time, in dragon form. Only now, I'll be coming on a dragon's back instead."

The thought of his arrival invigorated me. I wasn't sure I'd ever been as excited—or as terrified—about anything as I was about the coming meeting between him and Will.

Will would probably try to act daunting and protective. He'd test Callum in various ways, scrutinize him mercilessly.

But ultimately, he'd love him.

How could he not?

When I'd showered, I raced downstairs to begin preparations for the evening's visitors. I prepared a chicken for roasting, sliced vegetables for steaming, and I must have checked the freezer sixty times to make sure the massive apple pie I'd bought was still there, along with copious amounts of vanilla ice cream.

The anticipation of the coming gathering was killing me. But there was another emotion eating away at me, as well.

One that wasn't nearly so pleasant.

I still hadn't quite gotten over the sense of dread that had worked its way into my mind after my visit with the Graysons. A nagging, gnawing worry, about something I couldn't quite define.

Was I afraid I would find the boy they'd adopted, or that I *wouldn't*? And why did he keep wandering back into my head, like it was my job to think about him twenty-four hours a day? Why did I care so much?

With a sigh, I forced myself to set thoughts of the boy aside. It was Christmas Eve, damn it. Today was supposed to be about friends and family. A celebration of all the best things in the world.

I pulled the silver chain out from under my shirt and looked down at the Drakestone ring dangling from it, mesmerized by the illusion of dancing red flame in the stones' depths.

If Will saw the ring…if he knew what it symbolized…

He'd freak out.

"He'll get over it," I murmured with a forced shrug. "When he sees us together, he'll understand why I love Callum so much."

*At least, I **hope** he will.*

WHEN I'D FINISHED SETTING the table, I brewed a pot of coffee, sat down at the kitchen island, and expelled a long breath.

Will, Liv, Callum, Lachlan, and I would soon be hunkered down in the living room, laughing as we drank hot chocolate and recounted tales of our time apart.

It was a pleasant, simple fantasy. An image that should have been warm, reassuring, and easy to conjure in my mind.

But no matter how hard I tried to visualize the happy scene, I couldn't quite do it. It was almost like my imagination was a hard drive, and someone had deleted the file before I'd ever actually created it.

"Stupid anxious brain," I muttered. "You won't even let me *imagine* myself in a state of happiness."

As if on cue, I began to worry about Will. Was he in danger?

I thought about the plane, the snowstorm, every possible

thing that could go wrong. I found myself checking every few minutes to make sure his flight was still on time, that there hadn't been a horrible accident.

But each time I went online to look, the screen assured me that everything was fine.

Panicking about nothing, as usual.

After a few hours of self-inflicted torture, I texted Liv in hopes of distracting myself.

Hey, you busy?

~Not at all. Presents wrapped, parents bickering about dinner plans for tomorrow. I could use an escape. Should I come over?

Yes, please!

Within ten minutes, she was standing in my doorway, handing me a clumsily-wrapped gift covered in so much tape it looked like I'd need a chainsaw to open it.

"Sorry about the wrapping," she said. "I did it in thirty seconds. I figured it's the thought that counts, right?"

"It definitely is," I laughed, bringing her to the kitchen, where I handed her my gift: a new cashmere scarf I'd wrapped for her.

When she opened it, she gasped. "Vega! This must have cost you a fortune! I mean it must've cost *Will* a fortune. He paid for it, didn't he?" she asked as she wrapped it around her neck, caressing the soft surface with her fingertips. "I *knew* he loved me."

I chuckled. "Actually, I found it on sale," I lied. "You're such a good friend to me that I couldn't resist."

"Well, it's going to make my gift look terrible and cheap," she said, gesturing toward the tape-covered monstrosity. "But go ahead, open it."

With the help of a paring knife, I finally managed to shred the wrapping paper, only to discover a pair of hand-knit, multicolored wool mittens of red, pink, and orange.

"Holy crap! Did you make these?" I half-yelled.

She nodded. "My first pair ever. My mom helped me stitch them together, though. I hope they're okay."

"They're amazing!" I cried, pulling them on and giving her a hug. "I love them. Thank you so much!"

"You're welcome," she said with a chuckle. "I didn't expect such an enthusiastic response, I have to admit. They're just mittens."

"It's just…I haven't received a handmade gift in a long time. At least, not one so personal. It's a nice feeling."

"Maybe you can wear them tonight, to the tree-lighting."

"Absolutely."

"Speaking of which, I assume Callum and Will will be there?"

I nodded. "Will should get into town by four."

"And Callum?"

"Not sure," I said evasively as I pulled the mittens off and laid them neatly on the counter.

"You never really told me what happened with you and Callum, by the way," Liv chastised. "Why he left. Where he went so suddenly, or why."

"Ah. That. It's…complicated. I mean, we always knew he wouldn't be here forever. He doesn't have any real family here, for one thing."

"Yeah, but no one expected him to up and leave in the middle of the autumn school term. That was just weird."

"Sometimes things happen, Liv," I said, my tone more curt than I intended.

"Okay, but you're still together? Like, you're video chatting and having some sort of sad, long-distance love affair? Aren't you a bit young to bother dating someone you hardly ever see?"

"Sure, if you want to call it that," I said with an attempt at a cheerful chuckle. "But you know, with the internet the way it is, I feel like we see each other a lot, actually. It's almost like we're in the same room when we talk. It's kind of amazing, really."

"Well, I'm glad you're not too broken up about it," Liv said with a skeptically raised eyebrow. "Um—I promised my mom I wouldn't be out for too long. She wants me to polish the silver for tomorrow's dinner." With that, she rolled her eyes. "Don't ask me why my mother still uses the good silver, when we have perfectly good dollar-store cutlery. She's bringing out the fine china, too, like anyone will care about anything other than what's on the plates."

"I suppose it makes her happy," I said. "Maybe she just likes her traditions."

"Sure. Plus, she likes to turn me into her indentured servant, just to make sure I stay humble and don't enjoy myself too much. God forbid I should actually feel like I'm on *holiday* during the holidays."

"That must be it," I chuckled. "She's torturing you for her own sadistic pleasure."

"Tell me about it." Liv started heading toward the front door. "I'll see you tonight?"

"Of course," I said, following her.

"I'm so excited to witness the first encounter between Will and Callum. That'll be a hot-guy staring contest I don't want to miss."

"Ugh. Don't remind me. I'm slightly terrified that it'll all go horribly awry."

Turning back toward me, Liv snickered. "Just don't make out with Callum in front of Will, and everything should be okay."

"I think I can manage that."

"I don't know—you haven't seen him in months. I'd have a hard time keeping my hands off him, if I were you."

"I'll find a way to resist," I replied with a wink.

Little do you know how much time I spend in his arms...

I escorted her to the front porch and said a quick goodbye before spending the next few hours busying myself by preparing the last of the food for cooking, tidying the house and re-tidying it, and pacing the floor like some sort of nail-chomping maniac.

But no matter how busy I made myself, I couldn't shake the ever-growing feeling that something terrible was going to happen before the day was done.

And the worst part was that I knew there was absolutely nothing I could do to stop it.

THE TREE LIGHTING

I was sitting on my bed in the late afternoon, leafing through Mareya's book, when I finally heard the front door creak open, followed by the bellow of a familiar voice.

"Vega! You up there?"

Will!

I quickly concealed the book under my bed, raced downstairs, and leapt into my brother's arms, squeezing him so hard I thought we'd both keel over.

"I missed you too," he laughed. "I didn't expect such an enthusiastic greeting, I have to admit."

"Sorry," I chuckled, backing away. "It's just…it's been way too long."

Of course, he was oblivious to the fact that the last time I'd seen him in person was the day five dragons and I had freed him from the Usurper Queen's prison and left him, addled and confused, at the airport.

Seeing him now with a smile on his lips was the ultimate proof that he'd survived that trauma unscathed.

Through the open front door, I could see that the snow was still falling heavily outside. The entire town was now coated in a thick layer of marshmallow-looking fluff. Tree limbs hung heavy with layers of white, threatening to break under the weight of it.

It was peaceful. Silent. Perfect.

A snowy paradise.

Everything's going to be fine.

I strained to keep my voice in check as I looked Will in the eye and said, "Come in! You must be freezing. I'm going to make you hot chocolate with marshmallows and whipped cream."

"Sounds amazing," he said, running a hand over his hair to get rid of the layer of melting snow that had settled on top of his head. "I've missed this weather. Sort of. It definitely feels like home, anyhow."

He followed me into the kitchen, set his bags down, and sat at the island, staring at me curiously once he'd caught his breath.

"You look different," he said. "Like you're...brighter...or something. Is that some kind of makeup trick? One of those glowy sparkle things girls use these days?"

I lowered my chin and shot him a look of reprimand. "Brighter? Are you saying I was dull before? Wait—don't answer that."

"You were never dull," he laughed. "It's just...your eyes have changed color. Yes, I think that's it. They're greener. Or lighter. I don't know."

"You look different too, you know," I said, promptly transferring the focus from myself. "Like, you almost have a beard. What's up with that?"

Will scratched at his dark stubble, which looked like a few days' growth. "Yeah, I need to shave. Seemed appropriate for winter, somehow. I've been studying for exams, so haven't exactly had time to look in the mirror or worry about my appearance."

"Studying? Really? I would have thought you'd be dating every girl at the university," I laughed. "Or at least that they'd be trying to date you."

"Hey! I've been laser-focused," he insisted a little too forcefully before bowing his head and adding a sheepish, "Mostly."

"Ah-hah!" I said with a chuckle, handing him his hot chocolate. "So there *is* someone..."

"Yes, and maybe one day you'll meet her. Speaking of which," he added, looking around, "I believe there's someone you wanted me to meet? Where is this mystery human?"

Human.

Interesting choice of words...

"Yeah, um, he's not here yet. But soon. He'll definitely get here by the tree-lighting."

"Okay, well, he'd better not keep you waiting. That would already be a strike against him," Will said, bouncing his right fist into the left palm.

"You'll like him, I promise. He's very smart. Very nice. A perfect gentleman, too. He's...impressive."

"Impressive? I don't know if there's such a thing, at least where older brothers are concerned. If he's too good-looking or too intelligent, I won't trust him. If he's neither, I won't think he's good enough for you. It's a lose-lose situation, to be honest."

"Then we're in trouble. He's very good-looking and the most intelligent person I've ever met."

"Then I hate him already."

I sat down next to Will and blew on my hot chocolate. "How about if you keep an open mind until you two meet?"

With a sigh, he said, "Fine. I can probably do that."

"Good. You won't regret it."

TWO HOURS LATER, after more hot chocolate and a few too many cookies, Will and I found ourselves standing in the Commons, just as we had on the night of Midsummer Fest. We were both bundled up, Will in a down jacket, me in a long, dark gray wool coat, fur-lined boots, and my new mittens.

"There's Liv!" I said after a time, pointing into the distance where I could see her wandering through the crowd with Lachlan trudging along at her side.

When Liv spotted us, she grabbed Lachlan by the arm and charged at us, throwing herself into Will's arms.

"I missed you so much!" she yelled, pulling back to look up at my brother. "You look better than ever. I can't even believe that's possible."

"Hi, Liv," Will said with a crooked grin. He'd never known quite how to handle my best friend or her over-the-top flirtation, but he'd always managed to do it graciously, at least.

Will glanced at Lachlan with one eyebrow raised. "Who's your friend?"

Lachlan looked tired. Gaunt, even. Something seemed to be weighing him down—an invisible force, forcing his shoulders to hunch, his eyes to darken. His usual energy was somewhere else, and much as I could tell that he was trying to be sociable, I got the impression that he'd rather be tucked into a warm bed than standing in the Commons.

Liv introduced them, and I was relieved that she didn't refer to Lachlan as her boyfriend. The two young men greeted each other warmly, with Lachlan eyeing my brother inquisitively before shooting me a head-to-toe glance, as if reading him might give him some insight into what made me tick.

"Vega's told me a lot about you, Will," he said, his voice creaking slightly as he attempted jovial chatter. He threw another look over toward me, and I thought I detected a quick flare of something—anger, maybe?

But after a moment, it was gone.

"Oh?" Will said. "She's told me nothing about you."

"I'm not surprised," Lachlan replied with a half-smirk. "I'm an absolute pain in her ass. She's got far better things to talk about, really."

"You're not a pain," I protested. "Actually, I take it back. You absolutely are."

I would have liked to be able to explain to Will and Liv just how little of a pain Lachlan really was. How many times he'd suffered injuries protecting me. How much time we'd spent avoiding one another's eyes, or embroiled in intensely emotional conversation.

But right now, Lachlan looked as if he didn't want to be close to anyone. He had the air of a shy cat, looking for the best place to hide, to conceal himself so he could watch the world without being watched.

I found myself looking around, desperate to find relief among the gathering throng of spectators.

Finally, in the distance through the still falling snow, I watched the crowd part to let a tall, broad-shouldered silhouette advance toward us.

I knew without seeing his face that it was Callum. He was the only person I'd ever met who could silently command an entire crowd of strangers to part like the Red Sea to let him through.

Not to mention that there was no mistaking his confident gait or perfect outline.

When he was close enough, I sprinted over to him, leaping into his arms before whispering, "Come and meet Will. He's very curious about you."

"I'd be happy to," he replied, backing away and taking my hand. "Nervous?"

"A little," I replied as I led him back to the others. "Honestly, I don't know what I'll do if you two hate each other."

"Something tells me you won't have to worry about that."

By the time we'd reached Will and Liv, I noticed that Lachlan had disappeared. Distracted, I introduced Callum to my brother, pleased when they shook hands and offered one another friendly grins.

"How did you two meet?" my brother asked.

"Getting right to the point, huh, Will?" Liv snickered, throwing Callum a quick punch to the shoulder.

Callum and I looked at each other then blurted out a perfectly synchronized, "We met at the Novel Hovel."

"Liv introduced us in the summer," I said. "Callum was at Plymouth High for a while."

"Until he wasn't," Liv said, narrowing her eyes at him. "I can't believe you left us without so much as a word of warning."

"I had no choice. I go where I'm needed. Family obligations and all that."

Yeah, if your family consists entirely of one very large fire-breathing dragon.

"Well," Liv said, "I'm just glad you didn't dump Vega like the Charmers said you did. I don't think I could've taken her moping around for the next six months like some heartbroken waif."

"I would never dump her," he replied. "I'd have to be completely insane to let her go."

"Hmm," Will half-growled from his spot next to me, and I elbowed him in the ribs.

As a hyperactive Liv engaged Will in a conversation about his university life, I pulled Callum aside, ostensibly to look at a nearby spruce tree.

"Where's Caffall hiding?" I asked out of the corner of my mouth.

Callum directed his gaze toward the sky, which was still raining down a slow cascade of giant flakes. "He's enjoying a nice, leisurely flight," he said. "Somewhere up there, beyond the clouds."

"Good," I replied. "I feel bad for him—it has to be so cold up there."

"Don't forget—he doesn't feel the cold. I don't either, for that matter. I suppose it's an inherited trait."

I pushed myself onto my toes, kissed him on the cheek, and said, "You're right. I shouldn't worry about either of you. Now, come show my brother how amazing you are so he stops being an overly-judgmental weirdo."

Before we headed back to the other two, I glanced around. Callum asked, "Who are you looking for?"

"Lachlan," I said. "He's disappeared. He was acting strange. Sort of squirrelly. I'm not sure what's going on with him these days."

"Considering he's not my biggest fan, I'm not surprised he's disappeared," Callum said.

"Come on, he's not that petty. I'm sure it's nothing personal."

"*Everyone* is that petty," Callum chuckled.

Hand in hand, we headed back to the others. Will had just opened his mouth to ask Callum a question when an announcement came over the nearby speakers.

"It's time for the traditional lighting of the trees! Would everyone please gather near the bandshell so we can watch this spectacular moment together..."

We headed over to the spot where the entire town was gathering in a giant semicircle around the small half-dome of a bandshell. The snow had just begun to let up a little—enough that I pulled my cell phone out of my pocket in preparation to take a few photos of the spectacle.

Without further ado, the evening's Master of Ceremonies began counting down from ten as we spun around to stare at the dark silhouettes of the army of evergreens surrounding us.

I'd just held my phone up, ready to snap a video of the moment, when a text message popped up on the screen.

My heart pounding in my chest, I pulled the phone down and stared.

The sender was Kathryn Grayson.

And the message read:

I remembered the woman's name.

FIREFIGHT

AFTER THE INITIAL message came through, three periods bounced menacingly across my screen, taunting my brain with all the potential they held.

Mrs. Grayson, it seemed, was writing her next message. But what was taking so damned long?

"Eight!" the Master of Ceremonies' voice called out over the loudspeakers.

"Vega?" Callum's voice said gently from beside me. "You all right?"

"Seven!"

"I'm…"

A sudden chorus of confused murmurs echoed around me, rising quickly to shouts. It took me a moment to realize I wasn't imagining them.

Puzzled, I pulled my eyes away from my phone to see what was going on.

"Six!"

A bright orange flash filled the sky above us, illuminating the clouds in a ghastly, fiery display as baffled shrieks erupted in the crowd.

The countdown to the tree-lighting, which had just reached four, stopped in its tracks.

A sensation of profound terror clawed at my skin as a second colorful explosion lit up the sky, accompanied this time by an anguished, inhuman wail.

"What the hell was that?" someone yelled.

"What's happening?" a woman's voice cried. "Are those…fireworks?"

"I…don't think so," someone responded. "I don't think any of this was supposed to happen!"

The crowd's eyes were locked on the clouds. Beyond the darkness, beyond the still falling flakes of snow, flashes of infernal light shot across the sky. Fiery lightning strikes, lashing out from left to right and back again.

I pulled my eyes to Callum's.

"That's dragon fire," I said quietly.

He nodded. "Caffall's not alone up there anymore."

"Then who…?" I asked, my voice trembling.

"You know who."

I was about to utter the name of the man we'd seen in the Otherwhere's South when the phone in my hand buzzed. A feeling of roiling nausea overtook me as I forced myself to glance down at the screen once again.

Mrs. Grayson's second message sat in stark display in front of my eyes.

It was four words long.

Four horrible, sickening words:

Her name was Maddox.

ENEMIES

"MADDOX," I breathed, even as the town's population gawked at the still-flashing spectacle in the sky.

Not Maddox. Anyone but her.

My mind was already a twisting knot of horrifying theories.

Maddox was a Waerg. The head of a pack of wolf shifters who served the Usurper Queen.

…The very same pack who had taken Lachlan in when he was young.

My eyes sought out Callum's, which were fixed on me. Glowing bright, light blue, piercing through the darkness around us as every other set of eyes in town was still focused on the sky.

"Why is Meligant here?" he asked, his voice hoarse. "Why would he come to Fairhaven?"

"He's looking for his heir," I said. "Meligant knows his son is here."

"His son? What are you talking about?"

Before I could answer, something broke through the clouds above, shooting toward the crowd, wings outstretched like sails.

When a chorus of terrified screams broke out, Callum and I positioned ourselves protectively in front of Will and Liv.

"Vega?" Liv's frightened voice squawked from behind me. "What is that thing? And why the hell do you and Callum not look terrified right now?"

I held a hand up to silence her. "It's all right, Liv. Everything is going to be fine."

The silver dragon—Mardochaios, Suspiria had said his name was—came down for a hard landing, his human-sized talons clawing at the frozen earth as he hit the ground.

Some of the crowd pulled their cell phones out, no doubt hoping to live-stream the surreal moment.

Oh, crap.

Thinking fast, I turned and grabbed hold of Will and Liv, crying out the words:

Tempo cessat!

The rest of the townspeople froze in place, some in mid-scream, others turning to flee.

"I'll make them forget what they've seen later," I told Callum, releasing my grip on my brother and best friend.

He nodded toward the two of them, a silent question behind his eyes.

"I want them to see," I said quietly. "I want them to know it's real. It's time they learned the truth."

Callum nodded gravely, his eyes bouncing back and forth between Caffall, who still soared high in the sky, and the enemy who was all too close now.

Mardochaios stood some distance from us, his white eyes glistening in the pale light, neck curved in a tight arch as though preparing to unleash a fiery blow at his master's command.

Meligant, his expression blank, climbed off the dragon's back and down a bony protuberance on his wing, finally leaping stiffly to the ground. He walked toward Callum and me, his cold eyes fixed squarely on mine.

He was still dressed in what looked like decaying rags, his hair an unruly tangle around his face. He looked as though he might once have been handsome. Perhaps he had been, in the days when he resided among the living.

"Vega?" Will said, stepping up next to me. "What's going on? Who is this man, and why is he looking at you like that? Why is no one else moving?"

Instead of replying, I stared straight ahead at Meligant.

I understood so much now. Lachlan's strange change in demeanor since his eighteenth birthday. His sudden all-consuming desire for a family.

Meligant's hunt, after all these years, for the child he'd lost.

The two of them were craving one another. *Needing* one another. Some aspect of each of them had been reaching out, seeking wholeness.

Under any other circumstance, it might have been a sweet thought.

But if Meligant found his son—if they came together…

"You know," he said, his voice airy, almost a hiss. "You *know* who he is."

As if on cue, the snow ceased to fall, and the air went dry and still.

I stared at Meligant, my heart in my throat as I raised my chin.

"I do."

My worlds were colliding. My family—such as it was—was about to be torn in two.

And all I wanted was to stop it.

"Vega?" Will said, positioning himself protectively in front of me as Meligant drew closer.

But I took him by the arm and gently, silently, moved him aside, stepping into the clearing.

Caffall was still circling through the air high above the trees, his neck extended, mouth open, ready to shoot a ball of flame at his enemy if Callum gave him the order.

But I shook my head, asking him silently to go higher, to disappear into the clouds.

I'd lost my parents.

However horrible Meligant might be, I wasn't going to inflict the same fate on my friend.

I couldn't bring myself to authorize this man's murder.

Not yet.

"Vega!" Liv cried out as I stepped forward. "What are you doing?"

I turned back to look at her and Will. "I'm so sorry," I said. "I'm sorry that I could never tell you two about any of this. I'm sorry that you're finding out this way."

"Vega…" Will said again, but I turned my back on him to face the man who'd come to claim his heir.

"You should not have come," I told Meligant, my chest tight with fear.

"Do not try to keep me from my flesh and blood," he growled. "I *feel* him in this place. I have…seen him. Tell me where he is."

"Your son is a good person," I said with a shake of my head. "If you take him—if you…"

"It is not for you to say what I may do with my heir!" Meligant snapped. "He has been kept in the dark about his origins. He's been lied to. He doesn't know his true worth. It is time that he learned his fate."

He shot a strange, almost hungry look toward Callum, as if he either wanted to devour him or feed him to his dragon.

"You know him," he said, "Lord Drake. You know my son. You know that he has a claim to the Otherwhere's throne."

"The only thing I know is that you're a madman," Callum growled.

Meligant let out an enraged growl, inhuman and threatening.

Callum edged closer to me. I could feel his tension, his confusion, his rage, as he eyed the strange, hollow-cheeked man staring us down.

"Lachlan is good," I said, leveling Meligant with a cold, hard stare. "Don't destroy him with your twisted ambition. Don't do this."

"Lachlan is his son?" Callum cried, clearly shocked. "How long have you known about this, Vega?"

I held up my phone and showed him Mrs. Grayson's message. "Lachlan doesn't even know. And I didn't learn it until a minute ago, when I got this text. Maddox invited Lachlan into the pack when he was little. I'm not sure even *she* knew what he really was. If she had, she probably would have tried to use him, to mold him into something other than a Waerg."

"My brother was the Crimson King," Meligant said, his voice croaking out in strange, disturbing gasps. "And the blood of the great Sorceress Morgana flows through my son's veins. They told me my child died all those years ago...but I never believed it. I have waited for decades for this moment. I have suffered in silence, an exiled man in mourning. I have waited, and now I shall claim what is mine."

Meligant's eyes glowed bright, fueled by a dark rage. His shoulders and chest heaved, his fingers curled into white-knuckled fists.

I waited, breathless, for the inevitable explosion to burst from him.

"Tell me where he is!" he shouted, a surge of power crackling through the air around him.

"I don't know!" I replied, trying my best to hold my chin up in spite of my fear of the strange, hollowed-out shell of a man before me.

"Lies!" Meligant spat. He strode toward me, drawing a silver sword at his waist and stopping mere inches from my face.

My legs shook, my heart pounded. But still I managed to keep my eyes locked on his.

"I have not lied to you," I said.

He took a step back, a strange smile curling the corners of his mouth. "No," he said. "It seems you have not."

His head snapped to the left and my eyes followed, only to see a figure moving through the frozen crowd.

"I'm here," a voice boomed deeply in the night.

I closed my eyes, pain coursing through me like poison as I felt Lachlan stride toward Callum and me.

"It's all right," he said, taking my hand briefly, squeezing, then stepping toward Meligant.

"Lachlan, no!" I called out, but he merely shook his head and kept moving.

"I'm your son," he told Meligant with a certainty that told me he could feel the truth of the words in his bones.

"Lachlan!" I cried again, reaching futilely for him.

He turned and looked at me, an expression of sheer calm on his features.

"He's my father, Vega," he said. "He's the answer I've been looking for."

"No. You don't know him. He's cruel. He's not going to give you a nice home—he wants…"

Lachlan shook his head. "It doesn't matter," he hissed.

"My son. You think yourself a Waerg," Meligant said. "They've told you that's all you are. But you know better, don't you? You know you're more than a mere wolf shifter. Your blood is that of kings. Let me show you what you can be."

Meligant raised a hand, palm out, and to my horror, Lachlan transformed into a large, dark-colored bird—an eagle of some kind.

He took off for the sky, flapping his wings hard, but after a few seconds, the bird came crashing to the ground, only to thrash around in a desperate attempt to regain control over his body, which had begun shifting rapidly into different shapes. A snake. A bear. A small dragon. A hawk.

Each time he shifted, I heard what sounded like a small, faraway scream of pain.

"Stop it!" I shouted. "You'll kill him!"

"He is strong," Meligant said with a twisted smile. "He will learn to control it. He will learn to command his body and mind, just as he will learn to command armies. This is only the beginning for my son." He looked down at Lachlan, still thrashing on the ground, clearly exhausted by the effort to regain control. "I will show you what you truly are. You will soon see that you are more powerful than any other living man. More powerful than the Usurper Queen, or that warlock husband of hers. More powerful than any wizard. And more powerful than..." A chill passed over my skin as his eyes focused on Callum. "...the one they call the *rightful heir.*"

Nauseated, I struggled to remain upright.

I knew then that Meligant would never be satisfied with his son merely taking the throne.

He wouldn't be happy until Callum was dead.

I looked up into the sky, hoping my thoughts would make their way to Caffall.

This had to end, for the good of every single person in the Commons.

The golden dragon heard me. Opening his mouth wide, he shot down toward Mardochaios, who was still standing on the ground behind Meligant, his blank, unseeing eyes failing to detect the threat in the sky above.

A few feet away, Lachlan, his hawk wings still flailing, was trying to regain some semblance of control.

His father, in an attempt to prove his potential, had imprisoned him in his own body.

And I hated him for it.

I leapt forward, clutching at the hawk, trying to right him as a stream of flame shot from Caffall's mouth, hitting the silver dragon square in the back.

Mardochaios screamed in pain, and Meligant cried out as if he, too, felt the searing burn. He turned and raced over to leap on his dragon's back, unsympathetic to the agony suffered by the poor creature.

Go! I told Caffall silently. *Lead them back to the Otherwhere. I will do my best to seal the portal once you're through. I'll...send Callum as soon as I can.*

I watched as he banked and shot toward the sky again, with Meligant and his dragon close behind, surging into the sky in fractured waves.

After twenty seconds or so, they disappeared into what looked like a solitary, dark cloud, twisting with glowing swirls of eerie circular lightning.

The sky-portal.

When the shadow of the silver dragon had vanished through the portal, I closed my eyes and curled my fingers into my palms, my nails digging crescents into my skin as I summoned all my strength. I'd never cast a spell like this one.

All I knew was that I couldn't afford to fail. I struggled, pulling at the portal with my mind as if trying to lift a ten ton weight and straining against the impossibility of it.

Finally, near collapse, I opened my eyes.

"It's gone," Callum said. "The portal is gone, and Caffall with it."

"Are you all right?" I asked, looking up at him. "I know you two shouldn't be separated like this..."

He nodded. "I'll be fine for a little. I can still feel him—I can *see* him—leading them toward the Chasm. He's faster than the silver dragon. He'll soon lose them and conceal himself. But I'll need to go to him before too many hours have passed. I am sorry."

"It's all right. It's not your fault."

I looked down at Lachlan, who was now lying on the ground

in human form, his hand pressed to his head. He was dazed, but conscious.

I crouched down next to him, a hand on his shoulder.

"Are you okay?"

"I…I don't…" he moaned.

"We're going to get you to my house," I said, pulling up to look at the others. "All of us. But we need help first. And we need to be careful not to draw the wrong sort of attention." I gestured to the still frozen crowd.

Shutting my eyes, I mouthed a name, hoping my summons would be enough to bring her to my world.

A moment later, I felt her close. A beautiful woman with dark hair, dressed from head to toe in black, emerging from within the crowd to stride toward us.

She knelt down in front of Lachlan, cupping his face in her hands, and I knew in that moment that she'd seen everything. The dragon fight in the sky. Meligant's wretched abuse of his son. All of it.

"To think you were in my home," she said. "You were in my house. Under my care. And I did not even know you. But now you are revealed—and Meligant wants to steal you away again. He wants to corrupt you. We must not let him, Lachlan, do you understand?"

"He couldn't!" I said. "Lachlan would never…" But I stopped myself and looked around at the faces surrounding us. "The townspeople…they know. They saw the dragons. I need to make them forget."

"Then do it," Solara said. "You know how."

Swallowing hard, I nodded, turned to the crowd, and took Will and Liv by the hands.

Slowly, smoothly, I called out two words:

Conoit destruit.

I looked at Solara. "Is it enough?" I asked.

"We'll see," she replied, waving a hand in the air.

The crowd began once again to move around, turning to one another with smiles plastered to their faces, gesturing at the evergreens and ooh-ing and aah-ing at the display of lights.

There was no talk of giant dragons. No terrified figures cowering under the protective branches of the trees.

Only happy, blissfully ignorant faces.

"Well done, Vega," Solara said.

My sense of accomplishment lasted only for a split-second as Will stepped toward me, a look on his face that I hadn't seen in years.

It seemed that his former puzzlement was quickly morphing into rage.

"What just happened, Vega?" he asked, taking me by the arm. "What the living hell did we just witness?"

"My life, Will," I told him, yanking my arm away. "You just witnessed my life."

CONFESSIONS

WILL and Liv walked in silence between Callum and me as the townspeople continued to mill about between the Commons' trees. Lachlan, behind us, was moving slowly, Solara's supportive arm around his waist.

Watching Fairhaven's population continue their evening filled me with a quiet pride. The spell had worked. I'd done what I'd only ever thought Witches could do.

I only wished we could make Lachlan forget what he'd just learned, too.

"What are we doing?" Liv asked sullenly when we reached the edge of the park. "And who the hell is...she?" With that, she jerked her head toward Solara, who still had an arm around Lachlan.

I almost laughed. Solara was beautiful, daunting, and young-looking, despite her advanced age. I could only imagine what Liv must be thinking.

"I'll tell you more once we're at my place," I assured her. "For right now, though, just act normal. Give me one minute, and we'll be in our living room, away from all the watchful eyes."

"Your house is at least a fifteen-minute walk from here, Vega," Liv scowled.

"Like I said, just act normal. I promise you'll understand soon enough."

When we'd crossed the street, I ducked into a narrow alley, gesturing to the others to join me, and called up a door to take us home.

"Come on," I said, opening the door and turning to Liv and Will, who exchanged a skeptical side-eyed glance. It was only when Callum, Solara, and Lachlan had gone through that they agreed to follow.

When our entire party had stepped into the living room and the Breach had vanished behind us, Will turned to me, quiet anger still simmering behind his eyes.

"This is what you've been up to since I left town? What kind of voodoo weirdness is this, Vega?" he asked, taking a step toward me that was aggressive enough that Callum stepped between us and pressed a hand to my brother's chest.

"You can't talk to her like that," he growled protectively. "*None* of this is her fault."

"Don't you dare tell me how to talk to my sister!" Will shouted, the veins in his neck jutting out prominently. "Who do you think you are, coming in here and…"

Liv, meanwhile, had an odd look on her face. The sullenness from a minute earlier had been replaced with a look of wonder, of deep understanding…as if walking through the Breach had illuminated some part of her mind.

"Will," she said surprisingly quietly, as the two young men continued to bicker in the middle of my living room.

They didn't hear her.

"Will!" she shouted this time, leaping toward him and grabbing his hand.

He finally stopped snarling at Callum and turned her way.

"What?" he spat.

"I think I understand now," she said. "There are…things…that have confused me for months. You haven't been here to see it—to experience it. But I have. In a weird way, I get it. The dragons… the magic, or whatever it is. All of it."

"That's a joke, right?" Will asked. "You think any of this is funny?"

Liv shook her head, dead serious. "I don't think any of this is funny. But it all adds up." She pushed herself between him and Callum, putting her hands on his shoulders. "I've seen things— and I suspect you have, too."

"I don't know what you're talking about."

"Look into my eyes and breathe for a moment. Just breathe."

My brother did as she asked, but I could see from his expression that he was still annoyed beyond words.

"Will—tell me something, and be honest—have you had any strange recurring dreams lately?" Liv asked.

I threw Solara a look. *Dreams? What's she talking about?*

But the Witch remained stone-faced as she watched the two Worlders in our midst.

"I…" Will began, but he paused for a moment and locked eyes with Liv, his shoulders relaxing at last. "Yes—there's one dream that keeps coming back. How could you possibly know that?"

Liv ignored the question. "What are the dreams about?"

Will looked around at each of us, clearly embarrassed to reveal what had been going on in his mind as he slept. "Why does it matter?"

"It just does. Tell me. Please."

With a deep, calming breath, my brother said, "I'm imprisoned in something—some weird glass container, like a tube or something. I feel like I'm drowning…but I'm perfectly fine—sort of. Everything around me is a bit foggy. But I can see that you're there, Liv. You're next to me, in another container. I always know it's you, even though I can't see you clearly. And somehow, it makes me feel better to know you're there. I don't know how we got there, or why. But then I see Vega, pounding on the glass like she's trying to get us out. That's when I usually wake up."

"I have the exact same dream," Liv said, eyeing Will before she turned to me. "I've always just assumed it was my weird brain being obsessive about some subconscious fear. But it isn't, is it? It was real—that whole crazy thing actually happened to us."

I nodded slowly, my jaw tense. "You two were prisoners for a time," I replied. "Months ago, in the castle of a woman called Isla —known as the Usurper Queen. She took you captive to get to me. The reason you don't remember is that I gave you each a potion that made you forget, after I got you out with the help of some…dragons."

"Five dragons," Will breathed. "I remember now."

"When did this happen?" Liv asked. "When were we imprisoned?"

"In the summer," I replied. "Not long after my birthday. After I discovered the Otherwhere and…a few things about myself."

Without a word, Will turned, stumbled forward, and flopped down on the couch.

"You've been lying to me, Vega," he said. "You've never told me any of this. I could have died, and you never told me."

I walked over and crouched in front of him, drawing his eyes to mine. "Tell me something, Will—how would you have taken it if I'd called you in California to say, 'Hey, listen—I just found out I have special powers, and also that some psychotic queen wants me to join her evil army, and oh, by the way, she's using you to extort me. Not to mention that we have a secret grandfather who's a powerful wizard?"

"Grandfather?" Will shouted. "Are you kidding me right now?"

"Okay, maybe that was slightly too much information," I muttered.

Solara stepped up next to me and spoke in her smooth, lilting voice. "Vega's quite right, William. It's all but impossible for

Worlders—people like you and Liv—to comprehend what goes on in the Otherwhere. Hard to understand the magnitude of it—the importance of it to this world. It's especially hard to fathom that *this* world, too, is filled with magic users and creatures with powers you can't even see."

With the last few words, she glanced over at Lachlan, who frowned.

"Powers that I never even knew about, apparently," he said.

"Powers that a Witch long ago helped suppress in you," she replied. "It would seem that Suspiria—the woman who brought you to this world—when she introduced you to the woman named Maddox, she cast a silent spell. One that your father shattered tonight. One that limited your abilities. It's why you were able to live as a Waerg, but you never quite felt like you belonged. Never shared the instincts of the other members of the pack. The bloodlust. The rage.

"Suspiria tried to subdue whatever influence Meligant's blood might have on you. Meligant was right about one thing—you are better than most Waergs. You are kinder, Lachlan. You're a protector. You are not a Waerg—but nor are you a mere shapeshifter. You are capable of much more than that. What your father did to you tonight was a cruelty. You deserve a chance to develop your powers properly, without the influence of a man bent on destruction."

"I don't know what I am anymore," he said, his voice hoarse. "I don't know who I am. I haven't felt right in so long…I don't want to develop my powers. I just want my damned life back."

I sat on my knees, slouching, devastated to see Lachlan like this.

For all the complications between my brother and me, for all the mental mayhem at work, Lachlan was the one who was suffering the most right now. The revelation that had just been thrust upon him was life-changing.

I didn't blame him for looking like he was in a state of utter shock.

"Lachlan," Liv said, her chin down. "I've always wondered why you looked at Vega the way you do. Why you two seem to have this deep understanding between you, even though I never saw you talk all that much. I get it now. You know each other better than you and I know each other. You're so much closer than I ever knew…"

"It's true," he confessed with a quiet nod. "We've talked a great deal. But it turns out Vega was talking to a stranger—a pretender. Someone *I* don't even know anymore."

"My boy," Solara said, sympathy shading her voice. "Come. Let's talk." She looked over at me as if seeking approval, and I nodded.

She offered her hand, and to my relief, he took it.

"I'm sorry, everyone," he said. "Sorry about all of it."

They headed out the front door, closing it behind them.

I found myself wondering when and if I'd ever see Lachlan again.

I could see that Liv, too, was hurting.

She feels betrayed, I thought. *Lied to.*

And it's no wonder.

"You've spent a lot of time together. Time that I didn't know anything about," she said.

"I—we—" I stammered. Oh, God. Maybe I *should* have made her and Will forget everything, after all. If only for the sake of preserving our relationships.

"We have," I finally confessed. "We know each other very well. And even though I didn't like him at first, he's…he's like a second brother to me now," I added, looking sheepishly at Will. "It's… sort of hard to explain. I never meant to deceive any of you. It's just that I don't entirely belong in this world. I feel terrible to have kept so many secrets, but there was just no way to tell you

163

two. Not without putting you at risk. After what the queen did to you, I was scared."

My brother dragged his fingers through his dark hair. "I don't know what to say. What to think," he said, his voice slightly calmer. "I want to be supportive. I want to understand. I just feel so..."

"Overwhelmed?" I asked.

"Well, yeah. I mean, how did all this start? When I left for California, everything seemed normal, and now the world's gone completely bat-poop crazy."

"It started *before* you left for California. The night of Midsummer Fest. Do you remember when I disappeared for a while? We were downtown, and you and Liv lost sight of me."

Will nodded.

"A Waerg—a shape-shifter—attacked me that night. The man would have killed me, if..."

"If Callum hadn't come along and stood up for you," Liv said, her voice filled with a sort of evolving comprehension, like she'd actually witnessed the incident. "Callum's saved your life more than once, hasn't he?"

"Yes," I said. "He has." I took a deep breath. "I'm what's called a Seeker. I was recruited by the Academy for the Blood-Born to help find four important objects—objects that will help our side in a war between Good and Evil."

Liv stared at me for a moment before letting out a stifled giggle. "I'm beginning to understand why you couldn't tell us any of this," she said. "Did you go to the Underground station and look for Platform Nine and Three Quarters? Did you by chance meet a guy called Voldemort?"

"Perhaps," Callum said, gently interrupting, "it would be easier to show them than to describe it all."

"Show us?" Liv replied, and I could see now that she was shaking. Whether with excitement or fear, I wasn't sure. "You're saying you're going to take us somewhere?"

"It's all right," I assured her. "It's somewhere friendly. Somewhere safe."

"I'm tired, Vega," Will said with a defeated sigh. "I don't want to drive anywhere. Besides, the roads are totally covered in snow. It's dangerous…"

"We don't need roads to get where I want to bring you," I said with a shake of my head. "No roads, no cars, nothing. All I need is for you both to follow me through a door like the one that brought us here."

Will and Liv exchanged a look, frowned, and finally nodded their consent.

"Okay, then," I said. "It's settled. Will…it's time to meet your grandfather."

THE ACADEMY

THE WHITE DOOR leading to the Academy appeared in the middle of our living room, the Sword of Viviane clearly carved into its pristine surface.

"Wait a minute," Will said as I took a step toward the door.

"What is it?" I replied.

"Where are these doors coming from?" he asked. He was trying to sound calm, but in his voice was a tense panic, as if he was still afraid he was losing his mind. "They seem to appear out of nowhere."

"I've been able to create them for a while. I know it's kind of crazy to hear, but I can conjure objects—and those include portals between our two worlds."

"What else can you…conjure?" Will asked, clearly both intensely curious and apprehensive of the potential answer.

"Anything. People, animals, walls, weapons. You name it. I'm getting pretty good at it, actually."

"She really is," Callum added in a show of support.

"You could summon me a drink right now?" Will asked.

"Sure."

"You're not serious."

I closed my eyes and called up an item, which appeared on the coffee table. A tall glass of lemonade, complete with ice.

"Can I really drink that? Or is it going to turn me into a toad?"

"Just try it," I laughed. "I promise, it won't hurt you."

Like he was following through with a trust exercise, Will picked the glass up and took a sip, then passed it to Liv, who did the same.

"My sister is a Witch," he said with a laugh of surrender. "Amazing."

Though there was a time when I would have been offended by the W-word, I now took it as a compliment. After all, Will and I had spent our youth speculating that our Nana was a Witch, and all it meant to either of us was that she was magical, special, mysterious.

And most of all, benevolent.

"Something like that," I replied. "But I don't feel entirely deserving of the title just yet. Come on, then. We have things to do. There's a lot to show you."

Followed by Callum, Liv, Will, and I walked through the door into one of the Academy's lovely, broad hallways, its windows looking out over the sea to the east.

Despite the protective walls of thick stone surrounding us, Will and Liv reached for each other like the floor might fall away from under their feet.

"It's okay, you two. I know it feels like a dream, but trust me. This is all very real. I wouldn't put you in danger."

I led them along the hallway, past a few of the Academy's residents: Zerkers in red, Casters in blue, Rangers in green.

A few threw us inquisitive glances while others looked downright hostile, as if they could sense the two Worlders in their midst.

Thankfully, though, they didn't say anything—probably out of fear of what Callum might do to them if they did.

I led my party down a few hallways until we reached Merriwether's office. As we approached, the door spontaneously opened inward, as if it had been awaiting our arrival.

The Headmaster was standing at the center of the room, his eyes bright as he took in the sight of our group.

"I knew this day would come," he said with a half-smile as I ushered Will and Liv inside. "But I must say, I didn't expect it to come so soon."

"Something happened," I told him. "I didn't have much of a choice."

Merriwether nodded. "Meligant made his way through the sky-portal that I opened years ago, despite laws against such behavior. Those portals are meant to be off-limits to anyone not allied with the Academy." With that, he threw a look to Will, who stepped closer, as though drawn to the tall, purple-clad man with the bushy eyebrows.

"Will," I said, turning to my brother nervously, "This...is our grandfather, Merriwether."

Will hesitated, then held out a hand. "I...nice to meet you... Sir," he stammered.

Merriwether smiled in earnest as he took the offered hand and shook it. "I'm sure this all comes as a shock, William. And I want you to understand that I have no intention of pretending to take the place of the grandfather you knew—the man who lived in Cornwall. I am merely an...*addition* to your family."

"Of course," Will said, turning my way. "Though someone is going to have to explain our family tree to me."

Merriwether chuckled. "Your grandmother—your Nana—and I knew each other in the days before she met your grandfather. We...loved one another. But for various reasons, we could not be together."

"That's so romantic!" said Liv, who leapt forward, grabbing Merriwether's arm in a way that made his eyebrows arch sharply, though the smile never left his eyes. Liv had a way of settling into any environment, and clearly her initial hesitancy was dissipating quickly.

She began an outpouring of questions:

How long had Merriwether been Headmaster? What did that word mean, exactly? Was he still in love with our grandmother? Would he ever return to our world? Could he make Liv taller with nothing more than a wave of a magic wand? Were all the teenage boys at the Academy magical? Which ones were the cutest?

"What say we head to the Rose Wing?" Merriwether asked when he'd answered enough of Liv's questions to make her stop rambling for a few seconds. "I believe it would be somewhat more comfortable."

"That sounds like a great idea," I said. "We could have a fire. And some food. We never had dinner, remember."

"Dinner," Will breathed, like it was a lost memory he'd just retrieved from the depths of his mind. "That *would* be good."

Liv took his arm, smiled, and said, "Lead the way."

As Callum and I paraded along the Academy's corridors toward our wing, Will and our grandfather talked. About Merriwether's younger life. About Will's and mine. About Nana.

The world had gone mad on Christmas Eve, but things were miraculously turning out okay, at least for what remained of the Sloane family.

I could only hope Lachlan was feeling as warm and fuzzy inside right now as I was.

But somehow, I doubted it.

A REUNION OF SORTS

AFTER A LONG, delicious dinner—one that Merriwether asked the kitchen staff to prepare—we convinced Liv and Will to spend the night in the Academy, in two large bedrooms one story down from the Rose Wing.

"A Christmas gift," Merriwether told them. "Each of your rooms is stocked with clothing, bathrobes, food and drink. Everything you could wish for."

"How can we turn that down?" Liv asked, nearly bouncing off the walls until a crestfallen look settled on her face. "Oh, God. My parents."

Merriwether let out a quiet, deep laugh. "Your parents will never know you were gone," he said, turning to me expectantly.

"Time passes a little differently in the Otherwhere," I explained. "Or rather, the Otherwhere controls when we return to our world. Which is how Lachlan and I ended up here for weeks in October, and it only felt like a few minutes back home. I'll go back with you tomorrow—which will actually feel like it's earlier this evening."

"That makes no sense," Will said.

"And yet I've spent a lot of time here, and no one has ever

known I was gone," I said. "I mean, there *was* a time in the summer when Merriwether covered for me and sent you some texts, Will…"

"What?"

Our grandfather shrugged, an uncharacteristic, comically innocent expression on his face. Will and I exchanged a look then burst into peals of laughter.

"Come. Let me show our guests to their quarters," Merriwether said.

He led us out of the Rose Wing toward a bare section of the marble wall, where he stopped and spoke the word, "Aprus."

The marble disappeared to reveal a winding staircase, torches bursting to life along its walls.

"After you," Merriwether said.

When we'd followed him down to the rooms he'd described, he left us, saying he had matters to attend to.

"I am very pleased to have met my grandson," he said affectionately as he and Will exchanged another handshake. Liv gave him a tight hug, thanking him for what she called her "very fancy hotel room."

"You're most welcome. I hope to see you both at breakfast in the Great Hall."

"Of course."

When he'd left us, we wandered around Will's room, which was more like another luxury suite than a solitary chamber. A fireplace, a living area, a balcony overlooking the sea.

We seated ourselves on the couch and the large, comfortable armchairs, and Will threw me an amused look.

"So," he said with a sigh.

"So…I haven't lied to you as much as you think, Will," I told him. "Promise."

"What *have* you lied about, other than…" Will gestured wildly around him at our surroundings, "…all of this?"

"Nothing, really. The truth is, I wanted to tell you both what was happening on the night of my birthday. But I was so over-whelmed…I felt like I was losing my mind. Remember that mask you gave me? The one with no face?"

He nodded. "I do. It was creepy."

"That was sort of when it all started. I could see things when I had it on. Things that made no sense. And then…I didn't need the mask anymore. It was like a whole world of magic opened up to me."

"And it's open to us now," Liv said.

For someone whose entire life had just been up-ended, she really did seem astoundingly calm.

"It is," I said. "I expect the world—*our* world—will look different to you two now."

"I'm pretty excited, to be honest," she said. "Does this mean I'll have powers? Can I make the Charmers' teeth fall out?"

"No," I laughed. "But I probably can."

"I can't believe you haven't. Or, like, you could at least make Miranda's chin break out or something."

"I have bigger things to worry about," I said with a chuckle. "But thanks for the idea. I'll take it into consideration."

Callum and I stayed for another hour or so, until a chorus of contagious yawns began to spring up from our small group.

Finally, we announced that we'd be heading back to the Rose Wing.

"You'll be sleeping in separate beds, of course," Will said, throwing me a mock-judgmental look.

"Of course," I lied. "I'll see you in the morning. Enjoy your sleep."

As Callum and I headed down the hall toward the stairs, I stopped.

"What is it?" he asked.

"I'm just wishing I could talk to Solara. I need to know Lach-lan's okay after everything."

"So why don't you just…invite her to our suite?"

"Invite her? I don't even know where she is. She and Lachlan could still be in my world."

"You're joking, right?"

"Oh. Right." I chuckled. "Sometimes I forget I have abilities."

"I love that about you," Callum said as we started walking again. "You really don't have a clue how awesome you are."

When we were back in the suite, I closed my eyes and called to Solara silently, hoping to find her unoccupied.

She appeared a few seconds later, a ripple of light, then a dash of black smoke, before I found her standing before me in front of the hearth.

"I hope I didn't take you away from Lachlan," I said.

"Not at all. We came through a portal an hour ago. He's in bed in the west wing. He's a little exhausted, and I can't say I blame him."

Callum told us he was going to follow Lachlan's example and get a little rest, and I gave him a grateful smile when he planted a kiss on my forehead. I knew he was leaving us alone so Solara and I could speak freely, openly, about everything coursing through our worried minds.

"Tea?" I asked Solara, who nodded yes.

I summoned a pot and two cups, and Solara watched with an "I'm impressed" expression, immediately reaching for her cup.

"Good," she said when she'd taken a sip.

"Is it? I wasn't sure how strong it should be."

"No. I meant, that was a well-cast spell. But you do know you're meant for more than parlor tricks, don't you, Vega?"

I pouted slightly, my feelings a little bruised. "I'm not sure I'd call it a parlor trick…"

"I don't mean to belittle your skill," Solara laughed. "I'm sorry. It's just that…there's something you're holding back inside yourself, as if you're reluctant to unleash it. You keep your talents hidden, just as your grandfather does. I don't know if you even realize that Merriwether is the greatest wizard in the Otherwhere."

I sipped my tea. It *was* good. Almost as good as the insanely delicious brew Solara had served the last time I'd visited her. "I've heard that he's impressive," I replied. "But he's very modest. I've never seen him show off or anything like that, so I guess I don't really know what he's capable of."

"He's dedicated his life—his entire existence—to making sure others can develop their own skills, their own powers. He is an incredible man, really. Some wizards are corrupt, rotten to the core. But Merriwether is the essence of hope for the future. He cares deeply about the Otherwhere. He wants what's best for this land." She let out a deep sigh, focused her eyes on the fireplace for a moment, then said, "Which brings me to my nephew."

"Your nephew," I repeated. So strange to hear her say the word. "Did you two have a good talk?"

"We did. Intense, of course. To discover, after all this time, that he had been right under my nose—that was something incredible. I can see so much of the world with nothing more than my mind. But he remained a mystery until this evening. Incredible."

"Whatever you did to push him from your mind worked, I guess," I said.

"It did. Better than I'd ever imagined."

"What about Lachlan? How is he feeling about everything?"

"Ah. That's a rather more complicated question, isn't it?" Another sigh. "He's confused, of course. How could he not be? To meet his father in that manner—a creature who was terrorizing your hometown. A heartless wraith of a man. What a thing, to realize *that's* your closest relative. Lachlan is strong, but he'll need to make some choices. He will be tested, and soon. And he will find himself changing, regardless of what he decides to do with his future."

I thought for a moment before saying, "Mareya told him once

that he was more than a mere Waerg. It seemed so odd at the time—almost like an insult. Now I understand what she was talking about."

Solara nodded. "She was right. He's not just a Waerg—not that there's anything inherently *wrong* with Waergs. Lachlan's wolf, in fact, is simply one way in which his abilities manifest themselves. If he puts his mind to it, he will find that he can take on many forms. But he can't rush his development. His father was trying to force the gifts out of him tonight, but he did so aggressively, cruelly."

"You're saying Lachlan is a shape-shifter?"

"Among other things, yes. Like another man you know."

"Lumus, you mean," I said, recalling the sadistic warlock husband of the Usurper Queen. "Wait—are you saying Lachlan is a *warlock?*"

"No. Lachlan is something indefinable," Solara said. "He has a magic within him—the magic of a Witch on one side, and a dragon shifter on the other—that could be used for good or ill. At the moment he's balancing on a very narrow tightrope. And whether he admits it or not, he is tempted by his father's plan for his future. A future that, at the very least, would be exciting. It would give him the purpose he's been craving."

"Tempted?" I asked. "I can't imagine that for a second. Lachlan is so...not like Meligant. He's the opposite. He doesn't even *look* like him. Actually, he looks more like you."

"He may take after my side of the family, but his father's blood still runs through his veins. And because of it, he has a bumpy road ahead of him. Remember, he was raised by Waergs who work in the service of the Usurper Queen. He was taught to hate, to kill. It's a wonder he turned out so kind, really. So protective of you."

"I suppose that's true."

But I shuddered as I recalled a time when he didn't seem so good. When I'd first met him, I'd seen the mischief behind his eyes—almost a cruelty, like he enjoyed toying with my mind just as Maddox did.

But when he'd first had the opportunity to kill me, he'd protected me instead. Against all the odds, he and I had become close friends.

He'd overcome the cruelty that Maddox had tried to instill in him.

I liked to think that boy—the one who would give his life to help someone—was the true Lachlan. That his heart was an organ inherited from his mother, rather than from his strange, inhuman father.

"Power corrupts," Solara said absently before adding, "Lachlan told me he has always seen himself as a boy without a family, without a true home. I can feel a pull in him—a temptation to embrace his new identity. He knows what he could be—what he could *have*." She took my hand, holding it tight. "And what he cannot have, but nevertheless wants."

My skin heated under her gaze. "I'm only his friend."

"You are, and a good friend," Solara replied. "But you might be surprised how quickly men in positions of power decide they're entitled to the affection of the woman of their choosing—regardless of whether she's taken or not."

"Lachlan's not like that. Even if he thinks he's suddenly king of the universe, it's not like he'd become a total ass. He knows I love Callum."

Solara leveled me with a strange look. "He's my nephew," she said. "From all I know about him, he's a very good person. A good man. But I have yet to meet someone who isn't at least a little vulnerable to corruption. It takes a certain kind of strength to rise above the easy allure of cruelty and rabid ambition."

"Well, I won't let him become cruel. I'll talk to him—every day, if I need to. I'll tell him…"

"I'm sure you will," she said gently. She lowered her eyes, her hand still holding mine. "I was hoping I could persuade him to stay in the Otherwhere, perhaps even come live with me in Aradia. For a little while, at least."

"He can't!" I blurted out.

Solara pulled her chin up and stared at me, amused.

"It's all right," she said. "He declined my offer."

"I mean, I'm sure he'd be happy there, and it would be great for you two to spend time together. It's just…Liv…and I…would miss him."

"Of course." Solara tensed for a moment, then fixed her eyes on mine, and said, "He's in danger, Vega. More than you know. He needs to learn to harness what's inside him—powers he never knew he had, that could overwhelm him. He has a difficult road ahead. You need to prepare yourself for a different Lachlan—one you may not even recognize."

"I'll try to keep an eye on him, if only from a distance."

"Thank you. Ultimately, his destiny is his to command. But Meligant may try to influence him, to get his claws into him. He has ways of reaching across worlds—and I know from all too much experience that, empty and cruel as he is, he can be a very persuasive man."

I nodded, my eyes locked on the flickering flames in the fireplace, their reflection dancing on the sleek black stone behind them.

For a moment, I was certain I saw a face with a bright set of eyes locked on me, calling on me to come closer, drawing me into the fire.

Then…it was gone.

I shuddered.

"You all right?" Solara asked.

"Fine," I said. "But I think I should get some sleep. Will I see you tomorrow morning?"

"Possibly," she replied, rising to her feet. "Though I'll be going back to Aradia quite early."

I stood up, nodding. "All right. I…hope to see you soon, whatever happens."

"And I you," Solara said, giving me a quick hug. "You know, Vega…Lachlan isn't the only one who's spent his life in the dark about his true nature. Keep working on your spells. You may astonish us all—and, more importantly, yourself."

CHRISTMAS DAY

CHRISTMAS DAY—AT least, the version of it we spent in the Otherwhere—was wondrous. Snow fell from the sky in flakes the size of dimes. Out the windows, we could see the Academy's towers coated in layers of cottony white, which somehow made the ancient building feel even warmer than usual.

I knocked on Will's door at nine A.M. and offered to take him and Liv down to the Great Hall for breakfast with Merriwether.

Each of them was dressed in clothing supplied by the Academy's tailors: Will wore an off-white linen tunic and gray pants, and Liv wore a purple top and black pants that looked comfortable enough to sleep in.

"I have a surprise for you both after breakfast," I told them as we made our way toward the Great Hall.

"Where's Callum?" Liv asked.

"Preparing the surprise," I said with a mischievous wink.

"You're going to kill us, aren't you?" Liv replied, her eyes widening.

"Not today."

"What is it?" she asked in a comically whiny tone. "Tell usss!"

"You'll see. Call it a special Otherwhere-exclusive Christmas experience."

"Oh, good, so giant wolves are going to attack us."

"Not quite."

Will laughed quietly as Liv kept guessing for two full sets of stairs, all the way down several corridors, and even as we entered the Great Hall.

It was the Great Hall itself that finally convinced her to stop talking.

"Holy hell," she said, her eyes drawn up to our surroundings. The tall, arching windows. The series of lights, floating several feet away from the walls like dancing fireflies. The ancient, carved tables and chairs that looked like they'd once been used to serve kings and queens dinner. "This place is incredible!"

"It's home," I said. "Well...*second* home."

We seated ourselves at a table with a view of one of the Academy's smaller courtyards as well as the turrets and landscape beyond. Snow still fell in majestic flakes, but the view through the curtain of tumbling white, I realized as I stared out, was staggering to anyone who grew up in Fairhaven.

"I've almost grown to take it for granted over the months," I confessed. "It's nice to see it through new eyes."

"So you really hung out here every day in the summer?"

"For a few weeks, yes. I could tell you guys stories..." I threw Will a sidelong glance. "But I won't."

Best not to tell him how many people wanted me dead. He'd never stop worrying.

As we were chatting, the doors at the far end of the Great Hall flew open, and Merriwether marched in, energetic and bright-eyed. He headed straight for us, waving a hand briefly in the air toward our table, which was immediately covered in every sort of breakfast food imaginable: French toast, Eggs Benedict, smoked salmon, some kind of waffle that looked like it was made of dark chocolate, bacon, hot cocoa with what looked like home-made marshmallows…

I smiled as I looked up at our grandfather. Rarely had I seen him cast spells, and I'd never seen him show off. But this morning, it seemed that he was willing to have a bit of fun with his magic.

"Go ahead, before it gets cold," Merriwether said, taking a seat next to Will.

Seconds later, Lachlan came to join us. It seemed that Solara had already headed back to Aradia, just as she'd said she would.

I eyed Lachlan curiously, noting that he still had a shell-shocked look to him after the previous evening's incident.

"You all right?" I asked quietly as the others stirred up a conversation about the Academy's origins.

"Fine," he replied curtly before adding, "Sorry. I'm not fine. I'm…I don't know. I feel so screwed up, Vega. I don't know who I am. *What* I am."

"You're whatever you want to be, it seems to me," I offered. "The world is your oyster."

"I don't want an oyster. I can't believe I'm saying this, but I want my dull, predictable life back." He grabbed a soft-looking bun and took a bite before adding, "Last night I called upon my wolf, and he was nowhere to be found. It's like I've lost my strength. I'm paralyzed."

"No, you aren't. Look, I was the same way when I first found out what I was. I didn't know how to do anything, or what to do with myself. Hell, I'm *still* confused. But with time, it's gotten easier. It will for you, too."

"I just…I thought, for a long time, that I had it figured out. Yes, I missed having a family. But at least I knew I was a Waerg. There was a beautiful simplicity to it. Now, talking to Solara—*Aunt* Solara, I mean—it's like I have a world of opportunities opening up to me. But I'm not sure I'm the kind of guy who can handle that many options."

"Of course you are. You can handle anything life throws at you. I've seen you in action. No one has a better head on his shoulders than you."

"My father is an evil, psychotic ex-dragon shifter and my mother was a Witch," he said with a smirk. "That means I am, by my very nature, a mess."

"Only if you think it does," I said. "Besides, maybe your father isn't as evil as we all thought. It's not like he's gone around burning villages or anything. He's just…a little ambitious."

As I said the words, I could feel the lie in them. I knew with every fiber of my being that Meligant was cruel. He'd blinded his dragon—his other half. Who could say what he might do to his own son?

Lachlan ground his jaw and narrowed his eyes at me. "Do you seriously think he wouldn't have burned the whole of Fairhaven to find me?"

I pulled back, stiffening, and contemplated the question.

He had a point.

"He didn't, and that's what should matter here," I replied.

Lachlan was about to say something when a flurry of movement outside grabbed our attention.

"What the hell…" Will said, his jaw dropping open as two large flying creatures made their way toward the Academy, wings beating at the falling snow like they were playing a delightful winter game.

"Ah," I replied. "Our rides are here."

"Our rides?" Liv asked. "Wait—those look like…"

"Dragons," Will finished.

"They are," I said.

"The dragon that landed in the Commons last night looked like it wanted to eat the whole town," Liv said. "You're saying we're going to get *on* those things?"

I nodded. "These ones are friends," I said. "They won't hurt you. Think of them as giant, scaly golden retrievers."

"Last I checked, golden retrievers don't breathe fire," Will protested.

"And you're not supposed to ride them," Liv added.

"Fine. Giant scaly ponies, then. Let's go."

BACK HOME

Accompanied by Merriwether and Lachlan, we headed down to the eastern courtyard, where Callum and Caffall were waiting for us alongside the blue dragon I'd freed from the Usurper Queen's castle.

"This is Dachmal," I said when I'd led the others to his side. "He's the one who helped liberate you two from your glass prisons where the queen was keeping you."

"I remember," Will said, running a hesitant hand over Dachmal's neck. "Thank you, friend."

"I couldn't do it," I explained when Liv still looked too terrified to approach. "I wasn't strong enough. He and some friends of his are the reason you two are standing here today."

Finally, Liv sidled up next to me, put a hand on Dachmal's muzzle, and let out a low whistle through pursed lips. "Incredible," she said. "This is wild."

Will came to stand by us, looking into Dachmal's eyes. "So much makes sense now. About you. About this place. About our whole lives."

I nodded, wondering if he somehow knew how our parents

had been killed—that it was Waergs sent by the Usurper Queen who had caused the car accident.

One day, we'd talk at length about it.

But today was Christmas. A happy time. And all I wanted was to create a few carefree memories with my brother and best friend.

Sad tales could wait for another day.

When we'd said goodbye to Merriwether and Lachlan—who said he didn't feel up for a ride—Callum climbed up onto Caffall's back, while I mounted Dachmal along with Will and Liv so I could speak to them as we rode.

The dragons took us on a flight over much of the Otherwhere, following the route Lachlan and I had taken to get to the Northwest. We soared west over the Mordráth Wood, over the mountaintops and the forest that concealed the Aradia Coven. We flew all the way to the northern cliffs where I'd found Caffall and the wizard Marauth.

As the wind whipped around us, I managed to tell them stories about my time spent traveling with Lachlan. About his protective nature, our near-death experiences.

Naturally, I left out the bit where he'd kissed me.

I could only imagine how Liv would feel about that particular anecdote.

"Did you at least have a tent?" Liv asked. "It must have been freezing in the woods."

"It was," I admitted. But I chose to say nothing about how I managed to keep warm.

When we'd finally returned to the Academy, we headed back to Merriwether's office so that Will could say goodbye to him.

"I hope you come back very soon," Merriwether told him.

To my surprise, Will wrapped him in an enormous bear hug and said, "I absolutely will."

Liv, too, threw her arms around him. "Thank you for everything," she said. "This has been the most amazing experience of my life. I can't wait to post about it on social media."

"Um," I said, my eyes bugging out.

"Kidding!" Liv laughed, spinning to look at my face. "You should see yourself right now, Vega! You look like you're about to pass out."

"I'm fine," I semi-growled. "Anyhow, if you posted it on social media, your entire contact list would accuse you of taking hallucinatory drugs."

"True."

We headed down to the Great Hall to meet up with Lachlan. To my surprise, Will turned to Callum as we arrived and held out his hand.

"I'm sorry I was so hard on you," he said when Callum reached out and took the offered hand. "This has all been a little more excitement than I expected."

Callum chuckled and said, "I don't blame you in the least. I'm glad Vega has such a protective brother—but I'm not surprised. She's...very special."

"She is," Will agreed.

"Stop it, you two. You'll make me blush so hard my cheeks will melt off."

I sent Will and Liv into the Great Hall and told them I'd be in in a minute, after I had a chance to say goodbye to Callum in the corridor.

When we were alone, I gave him a long, deep kiss, and said, "I'll see you in a few days?"

"In a few days," he replied. His lips were curled into a tight smile, but I could see a world of worry behind his eyes.

"What's wrong?" I asked. "I thought everything went really well in the end...I mean, considering how things *could* have gone. Will likes you, and that's saying a lot."

"I like him, too." Callum looked over my shoulder into the Great Hall, where I could see Lachlan approaching Will and Liv.

Once again, Lachlan looked tired, like a dark shadow had been cast over his face, his eyes. "Keep an eye on him, would you?" Callum asked. "This will be a very difficult time for him."

"He's had a shock," I said. "I can't imagine all the things he's feeling right now."

"Lost," Callum said simply.

I stared at him for a long moment before saying, "You really care about him, don't you? In spite of his coldness to you…and everything else."

"I do. I suppose I see something in him…something familiar. When Caffall and I were battling internally, I felt an awful tearing inside me, like the battle between my two halves was killing us both. I can see the same battle unfolding inside Lachlan—one that he could well lose, if he's not careful."

"You won your battle," I replied. "He can, too."

"But I had an advantage." Callum drew his exquisite eyes back to mine and added, "I had you."

I turned to look at Lachlan, whose eyes, too, were fixed on me. I was sure I detected a quiet, lingering anger in his face. But after a few seconds, he turned his attention back to the others.

"He can't have me," I said quietly. *And it makes him angry.*

"He needs your friendship," Callum replied. "He needs you."

"I don't think I can give him what he wants, Callum. I'm not sure I'm *really* what he needs."

Callum said nothing more. Instead, he held me tight for a too-brief moment before finally backing away. "I love you," he said. "Merry Christmas, Vega Sloane."

"Merry Christmas, Callum Drake."

I watched him turn and head toward the Rose Wing, my heart full.

But as I headed into the Great Hall, a chill forced the warmth from my chest.

My eyes met Lachlan's once again, and I smiled, hoping to reassure him from a distance that nothing had changed—that we would head back to Fairhaven, have a nice Christmas, and things could go back to normal.

The only problem was that I wasn't sure I believed any of it.

"Are you okay to go back?" I asked when I'd sat down next to him.

He shrugged. "Sure. Why wouldn't I be?"

"Oh, I don't know. Maybe literally everything that's happened in the last day?"

"It's fine," he muttered. "None of it matters."

"How can you say that? You know who your parents were now. You have an aunt who's pretty awesome. It seems really important."

"Look, can we not talk about this anymore?" he snarled like a cornered animal, loudly enough that Will's and Liv's heads shot around to stare, confused, at him.

"Sorry," I said.

"What's going on?" Liv asked, shooting Lachlan a *what the hell* look.

"Nothing," I replied. "Everything's fine. Let's head home." I chanced another look at Lachlan and asked, "Good to go, then?"

"Why do you keep asking me that?" he asked sullenly.

"What is your problem?" Liv asked, glaring at him. "You're acting like a total douche-nozzle."

"Let's just go," I interjected, rising to my feet. "Maybe everyone just needs a little time to digest a few things."

Liv and Lachlan, clearly irritated with each other, nodded, their eyes down as I stepped away from the table and called up a Breach.

Mere seconds after we arrived in the living room of Will's and my family home, the front door opened, then slammed shut.

Lachlan was gone.

"He doesn't have to be such a knob," Liv said. "He was so rude back there."

"He's been through a trauma," I replied. "It's impossible to know how he might be feeling."

"I get into moods, and I don't treat people I care about like garbage."

"I think this is more than a mood, Liv," Will said.

I nodded my agreement. "He's dealing with a life-changing event. A moment where he's hit a fork in the road and has to choose which way to go."

For all our sakes, I just hope he makes the right choice.

TIME

A FEW DAYS AFTER CHRISTMAS, I found myself once again saying goodbye to my brother. After coming through a Breach into a quiet back hallway, we'd made our way to the check-in counter.

"Well, I guess this is it," I said.

"I guess so. Listen, if there's ever anything you need, just call me," Will said when we'd hugged for the third time. "Or... however you want to get in touch with your Jedi mind tricks."

I laughed. "Now that you know everything, I won't hesitate," I said. "I'm really glad, crazy as it sounds, that you're in on all of it."

"I am, too. Even though I'm still convinced I lost my mind on Christmas Eve."

We said a final farewell, and after Will had passed through the security gate, I finally headed home.

OVER THE NEXT FEW MONTHS, I continued my weekly visits to Callum at the Academy, which had begun to fill with with young men and women who looked like hardened soldiers. Occasionally I ran into Aithan, who told me he was running daily drills in the distant woods to prepare the younger Zerkers for battle.

Callum, meanwhile, spent his days working with Merriwether or traveling with Caffall to distant locales to meet with their districts' various leaders. He'd had several meetings with Kohrin, the Grell we'd run into on a mountaintop on one of our first ever dates.

"He's recruiting an army of Grells for us," Callum told me one evening. "Others, as well. They have many allies far beyond the reach of the Academy. We want to be battle-ready by late spring."

"Late spring?" I said. "Why then?"

"Merriwether has told me he believes that's when we'll need to make our first move. Don't ask me how he knows that."

I laughed. "I never know how he knows anything. But he's never wrong, so…"

Despite the constant flurry of activity, life at the Academy seemed calm, organized. Almost quiet. The hallways were filled with whispers between allies; the Great Hall was a place to confer in tight groups about strategy. Everything was done in secret, as if keeping details quiet meant the enemy wouldn't act too quickly.

Life in Fairhaven, on the other hand, was not quite so calm and orderly.

Each morning, I saw Lachlan and Liv at school.

Their relationship, which had always been a little strained, was now all but in ruins.

Then again, Lachlan didn't seem to want a relationship with anyone—including me.

I tried to talk to him several times over the months, occasionally cornering him after school in hopes of sitting him down for one of our intimate chats. Maybe, I thought, if I could get him to open up to me, I could help. If I could just get him to tell me what was on his mind…

But each time I tried, he snarled at me, his brows meeting, and told me it was none of my damned business.

Finally, one day in March, a knock sounded at my door.

I opened it to see Lachlan standing in front of me, a bouquet of roses in hand.

"What's all this?" I asked, perplexed.

He was smiling—an expression I hadn't seen on his face since before Christmas.

"I wanted to apologize," he said. "Could I...come in?"

"Of course," I replied, relief flooding through me like a cool, refreshing river. I hadn't realized until that moment how tense I'd become around Lachlan, how wary.

As I put the flowers in a vase, he watched. "I've been such a jerk," he said. "To you, to Liv. It's just...it's all been so hard. I wasn't sure how to deal with everything, how to process it."

"I can imagine," I told him, guiding him to the living room, where we sat down on the couch. "I mean, kind of. I won't pretend I know what it feels like to be in your skin."

"There's something else," he told me, twisting toward me. "Something I need to say to you."

"Okay," I replied, tensing once again.

Lachlan reached out and took my hand. I allowed it—it was a nice change from months of hostility, after all. Still, it wasn't entirely appropriate.

Even less appropriate was the moment he pulled it to his mouth to kiss it.

His chin low, he stared at me with an intensity that made me uncomfortable. His eyes seemed brighter than ever, his dark lashes accentuating their stunning color. I'd all but forgotten how handsome Lachlan was. How charming he could be.

But a shiver overtook me as I looked at him.

A warning.

"Why are you looking at me like that?" I asked.

"Because, Vega, I'm in love with you."

"God, Lachlan." I yanked my hand away, pushed myself off the couch, and scowled. "Not this again."

"I tell you I love you, and this is your reaction? Really?"

"We've been through this before!" I shouted, throwing my hands up in the air. "What do you want me to say?"

"That you love me," he replied, like it was the simplest thing in the world.

"I do love you. Like a…"

"Brother," he spat. "I know."

"It's not a bad word," I said. "If you only knew…"

He put up a hand to stop me, rising in one swift motion to his feet.

"I do know," he said. "I know everything I need to. I know, for instance, that I've bared my soul to you more than once, and you've rejected me at every turn."

"Making me feel bad about it isn't going to change anything."

"No," he said. "But there are other ways to change things, aren't there?"

"What are you talking about?"

He stared at me, ground his jaw, and finally muttered, "You'll see."

There was no question in my mind that it was a threat.

"What the hell is wrong with you?" I asked. "You're acting like you're entitled to me. This isn't you, Lachlan. I don't know who's in your head, but it's not the boy I know."

Lachlan let out a bitter snicker. "You still think of me as a *boy*," he spat with disgust. "It's no wonder you have no interest in me, when you have Callum Drake at your disposal. There are people who want to rid the world of him, you know. And it's very likely they'll succeed. Then you'll have no one."

He shot me one last acid stare before storming out of the room.

When I heard the front door slam a few seconds later, I collapsed on the couch, my face in my hands.

Lachlan had changed into someone petty, selfish. Unrecognizable. And in the process, I'd lost one of the best friends I'd ever had.

The worst part was that I had no idea how it had come to this.

DISAPPEARANCE

AFTER OUR HORRID ALTERCATION, Lachlan and I avoided each other for weeks. He sat at the opposite end of the classes we shared, disengaged from any topic the teacher discussed. When called upon, he would snicker derisively and refuse to answer on the basis that the chosen subject matter was "tedious" or "insignificant."

More than once, he was sent to the principal's office, which didn't help matters.

He fought with other students in the hallways, easily defeating them and breaking one boy's nose.

For that, he suffered three days' suspension. He returned at the end of it, completely unrepentant.

More than once, I contemplated going to see Solara, to ask her what I should do. But Lachlan's behavior, aside from being a bit bratty, was nothing out of the ordinary for a teenager. It wasn't like he was regularly turning into a dragon and setting the school on fire or anything.

Still, watching his unraveling was painful for me.

But for Liv, it was akin to torture.

"I don't know what's happened to him," she confided with a

prolonged moan one day as we walked home together. "I mean, yeah, okay, his father is some psychopath who rides a dragon. But that shouldn't have turned Lachlan into this weird, horrible juvenile delinquent. He's always been so...good."

"I know, Liv," I told her. "He's been more than good. I suppose this is him rebelling against his own bloodline. Rejecting his destiny." As we walked, though, I pondered my theory. "Or... maybe he's *accepting* it," I said after a time.

"What does that mean?"

"He's self-sabotaging. Setting himself up to fail. He doesn't care about his classes anymore. He doesn't want to be here, clearly. Maybe he wants out of our world. He could be looking for an excuse to go to the Otherwhere."

"So why doesn't he just leave? He could go to the Otherwhere anytime, right?"

"True," I said, puzzled. "He could."

I changed the subject to our upcoming exams, trying to distract Liv from thoughts of the boy we'd both lost. But the truth was, I was worried, too. It was as if some external force had taken Lachlan over. Cruel hands, grabbing hold and steering him in the worst possible direction.

It didn't take a genius to guess whose hands might be responsible for his downfall.

A FEW DAYS LATER, Lachlan failed to come to school. And a week after that, he still hadn't shown up.

"I've tried calling him," Liv told me. "Emailing, texting, you name it. He's not answering. Then again, it might just be because he's turned into a mega-jerk."

"Maybe," I told her. "Do you think he might have been suspended again?"

"No. I checked with the principal. He's just been AWOL. *Absent without leave*. No idea why."

A theory was forming in my mind—one I didn't like in the least.

When I'd charged through my front door after saying goodbye to her, I immediately called up a Breach to the Aradia Coven.

When Solara's door opened before me, I found her inside, waiting.

This time, it seemed, she had anticipated my arrival.

"Have you seen Lachlan?" I asked, breathless.

"Seen him? No. Not since Christmas."

"Is there a way to know if he's been here—to the Otherwhere —in the last several days?"

"There are ways. The Seers may be able to tell us. Or…"

"Or?"

"I believe you're in possession of a vessel," she said. "One with a dragon on its lid."

I'd all but forgotten about the small ceramic dish I'd acquired at the shop in Fairhaven—the one that had once belonged to the Graysons.

"You're saying it can answer my questions?" I asked.

"I am. If you wish to know where Lachlan has gone, the vessel can help. It's not as powerful as a Seer's stone…but it can give you what you seek." She stared at me a long time before asking, "What is it you're afraid of?"

"Lachlan hasn't been himself lately. Not since Christmas. It's like…he's angry. Lashing out, pushing everyone away. Like he's rejecting his own life."

"He may well be. But more likely, he's tormented by all that's going on inside his mind. I was afraid this would happen. That he wouldn't be strong enough to fight it…"

"Fight it? What do you mean?"

"He came of age when he turned eighteen. His powers, which

had allowed him to live the life of a Waerg for some years, began to grow and develop. And now, he finds himself filled with an energy unimaginable to most humans—one that must be harnessed, or he'll..."

"He'll what?"

Solara's face had gone deathly pale. She looked a million miles away, her eyes clouding over as if her mind was being transported to another place entirely.

Finally, after what felt like minutes, she looked at me and said, "You must go home. Look inside the dragon vessel. It will help you to find my nephew. It is of the gravest importance for you, for Lachlan—for the Otherwhere's future—that you do this thing."

I looked into Solara's eyes, which swirled with what looked like black smoke. In her irises, I could see movement. A dragon. A man. Flames and fighting...and for the briefest moment, I saw Lachlan's face staring at me, before it faded into a swirl of darkness.

"I can feel him," she said. "I can feel my nephew's mind being poisoned against all that is good in our world. He needs your help, Vega."

"Mine? But he doesn't even want to look at me. He'll never accept my help."

"He will," she said. "He must. Because if he doesn't...this land will fall."

"But what can I do? How can I possibly..."

Solara's eyes fixed on my left hand. My ring—the ring I hadn't worn since Callum had given it to me. On a whim, I'd slipped it onto my finger just that morning.

"It is an exquisite piece," she said, her voice altering to something strange, breathy.

"What?" I asked, frustrated that she wasn't answering my question. "Why are you commenting on a piece of jewelry when Lachlan..."

Solara took my hand and traced a finger over the swirling silver at the ring's center. "Do you know, Vega, why the middle has no stone?"

I found my body and mind relaxing with her touch, as if she was doing something to me—hypnotizing me, or…

"I don't know," I said with a shake of my head.

"It's waiting," she said.

"Waiting for what?"

"For the stone that belongs there."

She looked into my eyes, cupped her hand on my cheek, and said, "You've had it all along. The power. The ability. You've always been the strong one."

"Solara," I said, pulling away. "I don't know what you're talking about."

Smiling, she gestured toward my chest. I looked down to see that under my t-shirt, something was glowing red, bright enough to show through the layer of thick cotton.

The dragon key.

I pulled it out from under my shirt and off its chain, staring. The red stone at the dragon's center had never glowed like that.

Without thinking, I grabbed the stone with the tips of my fingers and pulled. To my surprise, it came away easily.

I pressed it to the center of the ring Callum had given me—between the two Drakestone fragments to either side, and watched as all three stones began to glow bright, as though a fire had sparked to life inside them.

"Do you remember what it was that gave the Scepter of Morgana its power, Vega?" Solara asked.

"The Drakestone I extracted from the cliff in the North," I said.

"That's right. But the piece you've just added to your ring is far more powerful. There are many magical stones in this world. Some allow the suppression of Magic. Some amplify it. The one you're wearing now is an amplifier."

"But the key," I said, staring down at the rather sad-looking dragon key in my hand. "I'm not even sure it would work anymore."

"You will find that you don't need it. It's a lovely piece, of course. But your skills have developed beyond its particular brand of magic."

"Don't need it? But how will I get home? I need to open a Breach to get back to Fairhaven."

"No, you don't."

My brow wrinkled with confusion. I wasn't into head games, but something told me that wasn't what Solara was doing here.

Was she really saying I could get home without a door?

"Go home, Vega," she said. "Do what you can to find Lachlan. Waste no time. And when you do find him, call on the strength that you were born with to confront him. Because I can assure you that he will do the same."

I thanked her and instinctively headed to the front door.

"You don't need to go into the street," she said. "Simply picture yourself traveling. You will soon find yourself at your destination."

I raised an eyebrow skeptically, but closed my eyes and did as she said, picturing my bedroom in Fairhaven. My bed linens, mussed from last night's sleep. My slippers, sitting on the blue throw rug. A red sweater, slung over the back of my chair.

My body went weightless for a moment, then weighted again, my feet planting themselves firmly on a hardwood floor.

I opened my eyes to see that I was indeed in my room.

And a whole new world had just begun to open up to me.

THE VISION

Desperate to find Lachlan, I opened my nightstand drawer and pulled out the dragon vessel I'd bought before Christmas. It was no Seer's stone, but it had revealed Meligant to me before his ominous visit to the Commons. Perhaps it could help me to locate Lachlan before it was too late.

Before I opened the lid, I stared for a few seconds at the ring on my left hand, its three red stones glimmering in the daylight. I was certain I could see fire dancing within each of the three—flames licking at the air, itching to fuel an unseen power.

My power.

Smiling grimly, I opened the vessel and looked in, focusing my energy on Lachlan.

The first thing I saw was a swirl of mist, dissipating to reveal a tree.

"Not helpful," I muttered, but told myself to be patient. Maybe the tree meant something.

It was thick-trunked, its branches fanning out to form a massive canopy.

"An oak," I said. "It has to be."

Still not helpful. There were a million oak trees in my world and the Otherwhere. This one could be anywhere.

As I stared, the tree came more and more into focus, its leaves changing from green to a deep red, as if coated in blood.

Beyond the tree, I saw what looked like the wall of a desolate stone fortress, with narrow, dark windows. Creeping green vines covered its façade, grasping at the stone like hostile fingers clawing at an enemy's flesh. I couldn't see a door, even. Whatever this place was, it was overgrown and unwelcoming.

"I need more," I said to the air. "I need to know if Lachlan is there."

In the bottom of the vessel, a flurry of movement, then I could see the interior of a large room with a long wooden table at its center. Lining the walls were silver weapons, hung with care, and a series of coats of arms, faded from centuries of sunlight piercing through the narrow windows.

At each end of the table was a large wooden chair...and in one of the chairs, a silhouetted figure was seated.

"What's that on the table?" I asked, squinting to make out the centerpiece.

The image focused and zoomed in, and then I saw it: a purplish sphere, swirling with energy, sitting on a silver stand.

"The Orb of Kilarin?" I asked. "But how...?"

The angle of the image altered, and now I could see the figure seated at the end of the table.

Lachlan.

His face was stern, his hands interlocked in front of him. He was staring at the Orb as if in anticipation.

"What's he doing there?" I muttered. "Where is Meligant?"

Just then, somewhere behind me, my phone blared out a long series of insistent beeps.

I recognized the pattern:

Text messages.

A *lot* of text messages.

I sealed the vessel and turned to pick up my phone.

Again, I was flummoxed.

Meg.

Oleana.

Desmond.

All three had messaged me at once.

As had eight others.

Each text came from a Seeker I'd trained with during my time at the Academy.

Each text message included one attachment: a drawing of a broad oak tree with red leaves.

And each text contained the same message:

I know where the Orb is.

TO THE GROVE

Breathing hard, I reached out silently.

"Merriwether," I said. "I need you."

"Come to me, then," a voice shimmered in my mind.

A moment later, I was stepping into the Grove at the Academy. The scent of orange and cherry trees surrounded me, calming my mind just enough that I was able to smile when I laid eyes on my grandfather. He stepped toward me, a grave worry in his eyes.

"The Orb has shown itself," he said.

I nodded. "The others have seen it, too. We need to find it."

"I didn't expect this for some time. Months, really," he said, his gaze distant. "It doesn't feel right…"

My heart all but stopped.

Merriwether was the most confident, calm person I'd ever met. He always had answers. Always knew what was going to happen before it happened.

Seeing him uncertain was terrifying.

"I don't understand. Are you saying what we saw isn't actually the Orb of Kilarin?"

He shook his head. "It is. It has slipped into the wrong hands...though how or why, I cannot say."

The wrong hands. Mareya had warned me about the same thing when I'd gone to see her in her shop in Volkston.

Merriwether was still speaking. "You and the others have no choice but to retrieve it, Vega. You cannot let it meet the fate Meligant has in store for it."

"What is he planning to do?" I asked. "What are you talking about?"

His eyes stared into the distance. He began to speak quietly, almost in a whisper...as if he wasn't addressing me, but rather some distant part of himself.

"It's why he went to Fairhaven," he said. "It's why he showed himself, after all these years. He acquired the Orb, and he saw his son in its depths. He saw others, too—others who are now in danger because of it. He knows a great deal...too much. He knows the past...and how to manipulate it."

I grabbed his arm and squeezed, hoping to pull him out of whatever strange dream was taking over his mind. "Merriwether!" I all but shouted. "I need you to look at me."

He pulled his eyes down to mine and smiled, cradling my chin in his hand. "I am sorry," he said. "I am so sorry it's come to this, my girl."

My girl.

"Come to what?" I asked desperately. "What's going to happen?"

"You must go. You and Callum both, along with Caffall, who must be prepared to fight. The silver dragon is a creature of rage, of treachery. His mind is polluted and festering. He will not be merciful. Caffall is the only one who can stop him."

"What about Lachlan? The Orb?"

"You will know what to do when you arrive. I...cannot say more. You will have to make a choice, and it is not for me to make it for you."

My heart sank. "Can you at least tell me where the oak tree is? The one with the red leaves?"

"It is a place called Entremer, on the southeastern coast. Callum knows it. It was once a residence of the Crimson King. You must fly there now." With that, he began to walk toward the far end of the Grove, and I had no choice but to follow. "It is of the utmost importance that you retrieve the Orb."

"I know that," I said. "But what about Callum? Will he be safe?"

"Callum is the most capable warrior I've ever known. He and Caffall work tirelessly, day in and day out, to master their combat skills. I am not worried that this will be his last battle."

"Thank God," I whispered.

When we got to the far wall, Merriwether waved a hand and a broad doorway opened. We walked through, and I accompanied him to the eastern courtyard, where Callum and Caffall were already waiting for us.

"The other Seekers," I said, turning to Merriwether. "They know where the Orb is, too."

"They are awaiting your signal," he said. "They know the importance of this mission. They will come when called."

When we reached Callum, Merriwether put a hand on his shoulder. "Do what needs to be done."

Callum nodded.

As always, Merriwether's instructions were cryptic, confusing.

But even worse, they sounded ominous.

I stepped over to Callum, who was dressed in light mail under his dark gray tunic. I threw my arms around him. He held me silently for a few seconds before pulling away and saying, "We do need to go."

"I know," I said, dread ravaging my insides. "Callum...I have a really bad feeling about this."

"Me, too."

We said nothing more as we climbed onto Caffall's shoulders and the golden dragon took off into the sky above, twisting southward.

It was some time before Callum finally said, "Merriwether filled me in on everything. I know Lachlan is with his father. I know what we're up against."

I nodded, the surface of my skin tingling with fear.

"You need to protect yourself," he added. "No matter what it takes. Lachlan won't welcome you with open arms. Meligant has probably poisoned his mind in the same way he's poisoned his dragon's."

"You really think he'd try to hurt me?"

"I don't know, Vega. But I do know you. You care about Lachlan, and you'll do everything in your power to protect him. I'm asking you to look after your own needs first. He may be too far gone to help."

I fell silent then. It had occurred to me that Meligant might want to hurt me—that he might be luring me into a trap with the Orb.

But Lachlan?

As surly and bitter as he'd been over the last several months, surely he didn't wish me harm.

"I'll look after myself," I promised. "But you…"

"I have Caffall," Callum said. "He and I are ready to confront Meligant, if it should come to that."

"Something tells me it will."

We fell silent for some time, until Caffall's voice finally barreled through our minds.

~We are close. I feel that he is near.

"He?" I said. "You mean…"

~Mardochaios. The silver beast. I feel him on the air.

Sure enough, a minute or so later, a large winged creature emerged from a bank of clouds in the distance, its scales reflecting the sunlight in blinding flashes of light.

"I see the castle...there," I said, pointing toward a large stone structure far below. My eye was drawn to a splash of red in one of its enclosed courtyards. "There's the oak tree. I need to get down there."

~*I can attempt to land, but there's a risk Meligant will follow. It could be dangerous.*

"No need to land," I said. "I can get there on my own."

"Vega," Callum warned. "You can't summon a Breach from Caffall's back."

"I know that, silly," I said, trying desperately to lighten the mood for both our sakes. I twisted around to kiss his cheek and held up my left hand. The three stones on my ring lit up like red-hot embers, giving me a swell of much-needed confidence.

"You're wearing it," Callum said with the biggest grin I'd ever seen. "And you've added a third stone?"

"I did. This ring—the ring that symbolizes how much you and I love each other—is how I know I can make it down there." I nodded toward the ground far below, and felt Callum instinctively grip me harder. "It's all right," I laughed. "I'm not about to jump. I have other ways."

"How...?"

"Trust me?"

"Of course."

"Then let me go. And stay safe. You too, Caffall," I added with a pat to the dragon's neck.

~*I will do my best, Seeker. Good luck to you.*

"Thanks. Something tells me I'll need it."

THE CASTLE ON THE COAST

STILL FEELING Callum's touch on my skin, I found myself standing among the roots of the ancient oak tree I'd seen in the dragon vessel, its red leaves bending toward me in the breeze, as if contemplating reaching out to touch me.

The castle, covered as it was in a sea of invasive ivy, looked as though it hadn't been occupied in generations.

I pulled my eyes to the sky, where I could see the two dragons high overhead. Already, they were locked in a standoff hundreds of feet from one another, treading air as a human treads water.

Each, it seemed, was waiting for the other to make a move.

"Please," I breathed, staring up at Caffall. "Don't you dare die."

As much as I wanted to watch the inevitable firefight, to watch Callum emerge victorious—the thought of the alternative was horrifying.

I commanded myself to get inside the grim castle, to find what I'd come looking for. Better that than watching the aerial battle in horror.

I closed my eyes and pictured the room I'd seen at the bottom of the dragon vessel. The Orb, sitting at the center of a long table.

Lachlan, seated at one end. Silver weapons and coats of arms adorning the walls.

And then I felt myself floating, my body nothing more than a feather, blown by a breeze into another place.

When I felt my feet hit solid ground, I breathed again.

"Hello, Vega."

The voice was unmistakable. I'd heard it a thousand times in a hundred different moods.

Lachlan Sinclair.

An invented name for a boy who would lead a reinvented life.

I opened my eyes to see that I was standing at the opposite end of the table from him. The Orb of Kilarin, in all its glory, glowed and rotated slowly several feet away, just waiting to be claimed.

"Hello, Lachlan," I said. "How long have you been here?"

Lachlan rose to his feet, an eerie grin on his lips.

"Some days," he replied. "You know how time flies when one comes to the Otherwhere."

"Some days," I repeated. "Days spent with…him."

Lachlan nodded, side-stepping to his left. I could see now that he was dressed in leather armor—a brigandine, tapered at the waist. A baldric, complete with an array of blades tucked into its small sheaths. He wore leather boots and linen trousers. But his arms, muscular and powerful, were bare.

He'd grown since I'd last seen him—not in height so much as in brawn.

"You look well," I said.

I didn't want to say "good." The truth was, he *didn't* look good, not to me. He looked like a quiet, simmering rage was on the verge of boiling up inside him, and there was nothing attractive in it.

"I've been learning to harness my abilities," he said, "thanks to my father. He has taught me many things."

With that, he took a step in my direction.

"Things? Such as?"

"Such as my rightful destiny," he replied. Another step.

A crooked smile brought out a dimple on his left cheek, and for a second, he looked almost innocent.

"I always wondered what would happen with us—with you and me—if I was something more than just a Waerg," he said. "If I was of noble blood, like your Callum." He raised his eyes to the ceiling and pointed upward. "They're going at it right now," he said with a strange, ominous click of his tongue. "My father is not fond of your Callum, you know."

"I've noticed," I replied.

"Here's the thing," Lachlan said, taking another step, then another, until he'd reached the Orb. "I've learned of the power of this particular Relic." He turned to look at it. "I've learned that it can be used to see through time."

He swept a hand over the sphere, as I'd seen Mareya do with the Seer's stone in her shop, and the Orb swirled to life, a sort of manic animation lighting it from the inside.

I stared at the moving images in the sphere's depths. Even from a distance, I could see what looked like Solara, kneeling by the bedside of a young woman who had to be her sister, Tarrah.

The young woman looked pale, her skin glistening as though she were covered in perspiration.

She appeared frightened, panicked. But she seemed too weak to fight whatever demon was tearing away at her mind.

"My mother," Lachlan said. "After she was stolen from my father."

"She wasn't stolen," I said. "Your father was cruel to her. He was abusive. He wanted you—"

"Yes," Lachlan said in a voice that wasn't entirely his. "He *wanted* me. And your Witch friends made sure he'd never know me, didn't they?"

Something inside my chest wrenched like a fist clutching at my heart. This wasn't Lachlan—this hatred of Witches, this bitterness. The Lachlan I knew was emotional, passionate, but kind and loving.

He wasn't hateful.

What I saw before me, I had no doubt, was his father, speaking through him.

"Meligant has sunk his claws into you," I snapped. "He's gotten into your mind. You know Solara only ever wanted to protect you."

"Did she?" Lachlan asked.

He flicked his hand over the Orb again, and this time, another scene appeared.

It was him and me, sitting in the woods by a fire, talking intimately, smiles on our faces. "So why did she sit back and do nothing, while I endured emotional torment?"

"What are you talking about?"

"I risked my life for you, Vega. I traveled hundreds of miles across the Otherwhere...for you. All for what? To come close to dying, while you went back to your precious Callum. Solara gave me away. She stole my life from me. My *rightful* life. I was meant to be a prince, and then a king. She ensured that I would become nothing more than a reluctant servant to the Usurper Queen. A minion in a pack of Waergs hardly fit to lick anyone's boots."

"She had nothing to do with you ending up with Maddox," I snarled defensively. "And you know it."

"She abandoned me!" he shouted loudly enough that I winced. The roar of his voice was inhuman, something I'd only ever detected on the howls of beasts.

"What would you have me do about it?" I asked. "Do you think I can change the past? This anger of yours—it's not going to solve anything."

"Perhaps not. But as for altering the past..." Lachlan said, shooting another look at the Orb. "That is to be seen."

"Look, I don't know what you're planning on doing…"

Lachlan assaulted me then with a smile that came from some-where else—somewhere dark and awful. Waving a hand over the Orb, he summoned me closer, and I found myself moving in, a need growing in my mind to see what images he was conjuring.

Did this power of his come from Meligant's side, or from his mother? What, exactly, was he hoping to do?

When I was a few feet from him, I looked at the Orb, which was twisting with familiar sights: Fairhaven. Our backyard. Will, as a child.

My mother, looking down at me.

"What—" I croaked.

Time seemed to speed up then, and I could see my parents getting into the car and driving down a road just outside of town.

Oh…no.

Wolves, running in front of them, the car swerving…

"Stop!" I shouted, lunging at Lachlan. "Stop this!"

"They died," he said simply, as if he was describing the color of someone's shirt.

"I know they died! What the hell makes you think I want to watch it?"

I could have killed him. Wrapped my hands around his throat and squeezed the life out of him, for what he was doing to me.

But all I could think was, *This isn't you. You're not cruel. This is some creature of pure malice, working through you.*

"You never have to see their deaths again," he said. "Not even in your mind's eye. What if I told you I could bring your parents back?"

"What are you talking about?"

"Vega," he replied, his tone sweet now, soft and buttery as he stepped toward me and cupped my cheeks in his hands. He smiled, but it wasn't the silly, charming Lachlan smile I'd come to know. In his eyes, I saw a twisting, black cloud, like a malevolent parasite had taken over his mind. "I can bring you back in time—

to that day. You can stop them getting in the car. Don't you see? We can change the course of history, together. You never need to lose your parents."

My mouth went dry. The idea of it—the notion that all that pain could be wiped away—it was as enticing as I imagined the most powerful drug in the world must be.

"You never need to experience any of it," Lachlan said. Then, his eyes locked on mine, he called out, "Guard!"

Almost instantly, the doors at the far end of the room opened, and a large, armor-clad man came marching in, dragging a woman with him.

I gasped when I saw the three parallel scars running along her left cheek.

Suspiria.

Her hands were shackled with a device fashioned out of some sort of gleaming silver metal. She was pale, with dark circles under her eyes, and she staggered as she moved as though she'd been drugged, or worse.

"What's she doing here?" I asked. "What is this?"

"My father found her," Lachlan said. "In his search for me. He told me something kind of amusing about her. Do you want to hear?"

"No!" I snapped. "I want you to let her go."

Lachlan ignored my demand. "She has an ability to travel through time," he said, "and to bring others with her."

"I know. But surely you can't be planning to force her…"

My jaw dropped, and I froze.

Yes. That was exactly what he was planning.

The Orb began to swirl again, this time with new images: Me, hanging out with Liv in the hallway at school. Time spent with Will over the years.

On my seventeenth birthday, walking into the Novel Hovel and coming face to face with Callum for the very first time.

My heart leapt as I looked at him and remembered the purity

of that first instant. The first moment I'd ever laid eyes on him. The instant ache of desire I'd felt for the boy I'd never met.

"This is what it's all about," I breathed, glaring at Lachlan. "You want to erase Callum from my life."

"I want to give you your family back. Callum would simply be a casualty of your happiness."

I leveled Lachlan with a look of pure rage. "You don't care about my family. You want to erase everything I've felt. The love I feel for Callum. The completion I feel *because* of him. The healing, the wholeness. You would take him from me. You would take Merriwether, my grandfather, my flesh and blood, from me, too."

"I would never do that, Vega."

"If you take Callum, you take it all. You take my powers, my true nature. You take my life from me, Lachlan. Don't you see? Callum is the key to it all. Meeting him—knowing him—is what's made me strong enough to endure all of this. As much as I want my parents back, I can't let you erase the lives of so many people. It would be wrong. It would be cruel."

"It would be right!" he growled. "If I could go back and be raised by my father—Don't you see? You don't need Callum. You could be strong with *me*."

Ah, I thought. *So that's what it comes down to.*

A selfish desire from a selfish boy.

I shook my head, my fingers curling into my palms, fists tight as steel. "I wouldn't be strong with you," I said. "I would be weak, and cruel. In a matter of days, your father has turned you into someone I don't even recognize. Who knows that he'd do to me?" I looked at Suspiria, who was leaning against the guard, her breath heavy. I finally understood why she'd lied to me when we'd met about seeing the Graysons more than once.

She'd been terrified that Meligant would find her. That he would find out she'd helped steer his heir toward a life with a pack of Waergs.

"Meligant," I said, glaring at Lachlan, "has turned you into someone who ensnares innocent women to use them for your own selfish purposes."

Without even thinking, I shot a hand out toward Suspiria and whispered an incantation. A word that I'd learned from Mareya's book, though I had no recollection of it.

Libera Sorcela.

The silver cuffs disappeared from her wrists. The color returned to her cheeks, and she was able to push her shoulders back, the exhaustion seemingly leaving her body.

"Go now," I said to her, twisting my hand around and slamming my eyes shut. "Go…"

I pictured her back in Salem, in her shop. Safe…for a little, at least.

When I opened my eyes, she was gone.

Enraged, I stepped toward Lachlan, watching with vindictive pleasure as he took a step backwards.

"You can't take away what I am," I snarled, "or who I am. I won't let you. You can't alter my fate, just as you can't change Callum's, or your own. I was meant to exist right here, right now. Just as Callum is meant to sit on the throne. And like it or not, you know it, Lachlan."

"Fate is a malleable concept," he protested. "We control our own destinies. And I choose to control mine, which means I can choose to control *yours*."

I closed my eyes and said, "You will do no such thing. Do you hear me?" My voice trembling with anger, I turned to face the Orb of Kilarin and added, "I think it's time you handed it over."

Lachlan laughed. "You think I'd give it to you, just like that?"

I shook my head again, a smile on my lips.

"No. But I think you might give it to *them*."

With that, I nodded to the far end of the room where ten

Seekers, each of them dressed in the silver tunics of the Academy, were now standing, ready to fight for our world and for the Otherwhere.

LOSS

WHAT HAPPENED NEXT WAS a rabid frenzy of activity.

Lachlan let out a roar, and a dozen guards—large men in tarnished silver armor that looked as if it was meant to mimic Mardochaios' scales—charged into the room.

Two of them positioned themselves on either side of the table and crossed their weapons over the Orb of Kilarin. Their faces were blank and expressionless, as though they were possessed by something beyond their own minds.

"Desmond!" I called out. "Can you get them to move?"

He focused his mind on one of the two guards, then the other, then shook his head. "They're mindless," he said. "Or something. I can't control them!"

"What about the others?" I asked as a guard came running toward me. Crane, a tall, gangly Seeker, jumped in front of him, distracting him just long enough that I could leap out of the way.

"Weapons!" called Meg, who had already begun to race around the room at lightning speed, grabbing swords, pikes, and daggers off the wall and distributing them to our fellow Seekers. She threw a sword to Crane, who managed to fight off the guard who'd nearly attacked me.

Thinking fast, I clothed my allies from head to toe in chain-mail light enough that they could still move quickly. The Seekers leapt at the guards like seasoned fighters, wielding their weapons as if they'd never stopped training.

Some, like Oleana, cast offensive spells, sending the guards reeling backwards, only to attack again.

Desmond was locked in a staring contest with another of the men, digging into his mind, controlling his movements. The man —a dark-haired creature with a permanent scowl on his face— hurled himself at another guard, and they tumbled to the floor, limbs flailing, as they struggled to overpower one another.

"They're not all mindless!" Desmond shouted with a huge grin. "This is quite fun, really!"

Each Seeker was doing their part to take on the small army.

But the Orb of Kilarin still sat in the middle of the table, still protected by its two unmoving guardians.

Lachlan, clearly angry that my allies hadn't all perished in a massive heap of blood and bone, was standing near the Orb, staring at me.

As I looked into his eyes, I was acutely aware that he was the most dangerous person in the room. The one who had the most to lose if the Orb disappeared—and the most to gain if it remained.

Whatever else happened, I couldn't let him get his hands on it.

"Outside," I mouthed, rushing at Lachlan and grabbing his arm just as he reached for the Relic of Power.

A second later, he and I were standing at the base of the oak tree with the red leaves.

Okay, I thought. *What now?*

"I'm glad we're out here," Lachlan hissed. "There's something I want to show you. A trick my father has helped me develop."

"What trick?" I asked, swallowing hard. *Let him perform every trick in the book. As long as he's nowhere near the Orb of Kilarin.*

"One that I think you'll like." He assumed a casual stance, his arms crossed, and stared into my eyes. "You see, I was wondering why my wolf and I were never close," he said. "Why didn't I feel more of a connection to him, a kinship, if he and I were one entity?"

"I don't know," I said. "I don't care."

"It turns out," Lachlan added, ignoring my scowl, "that I have many skills, and my esteemed father has taught me to unleash them. Do you want to see?"

"Not particularly," I replied through gritted teeth. "But something tells me you'll show me, whether I like it or not."

"I will. Once *they're* done entertaining us."

With that, he pointed toward the sky.

High among the clouds, flames shot back and forth in an angry display as Caffall and Mardochaios assaulted one another, dodging this way and that to avoid catastrophe.

"My father will win," Lachlan snarled, pulling his eyes up to watch them. "Callum will be defeated, and you will turn to me for comfort."

I shook my head, a violent rage welling inside me. "No way," I growled. "Whatever happens, I'll never turn to you. *Never.*"

A shriek erupted in the sky above us and I looked up just long enough to see a bolt of flame pierce through Caffall's left wing.

"No…" I breathed, a shooting pain hitting me square in the chest.

"You see?" Lachlan said. "Your dragon lord isn't so impressive, after all."

Caffall managed to stay airborne despite the gaping wound. Recovering his balance, he hurled a massive fireball at Mardochaios, hitting him square in the chest.

I held my breath as I watched the silver dragon begin to tumble toward the earth, his wings flat to his side, his body spiraling out of control.

"He's done it!" I heard myself saying. "Caffall's got him!"

I pulled my eyes to Lachlan, who was smiling a grim, toothy

grin. Not the expression of someone whose father was about to go crashing to the ground.

"There are birds in your world," he said calmly, even as Mardochaios continued to plummet. "Tumbler pigeons, they're called. They learn to fall toward the ground, rolling and somersaulting as though they're wounded. Some say it's a tactic they learn in order to evade predators."

My stomach turned as I watched the silver dragon continue his fall, a perfectly choreographed series of rolls, like a diver leaping from the high board.

Higher in the sky, the golden dragon was flapping his wings slowly, calmly.

He thinks he's won, I thought as Caffall turned, flying in a broad circle above the castle, assessing where would be best to land. *He thinks it's over.*

"Callum," I said out loud.

"He can't hear you. But then, you know that, don't you?" Lachlan laughed.

Callum...

I spoke his name with my mind, struggling to send it his way.

Your'e in danger...

Sure enough, just as Mardochaios came within twenty feet of the ground, he regained his balance and shot like an arrow into the sky.

Callum and Caffall had their eyes focused on the distance. They wouldn't see the attack coming.

It's a trap! I screamed with my mind, hoping with everything in me that they'd hear me.

As I watched Caffall stop in midair and pivot, Lachlan lunged toward me, shifting in mid-step into an enormous, horrific bear. His canines jutted out of his mouth like daggers. His lips were curled back in a feral snarl. His eyes were jet-black, swirling with reels of onyx smoke.

He was coming at me, one enormous paw in front of the other.

"This isn't you, Lachlan," I found myself saying as I backed away.

His claws were as large and as sharp as daggers, each one capable of ending me. With one bite of his jaw, my neck would snap. I should have found him terrifying.

Yet all I felt was sadness.

"You don't want to do this, Lachlan," I pleaded. "You're not a killer."

My words only served to accelerate his pace. I jogged backwards, futilely hoping to avoid a physical altercation.

Above us, a crack like thunder sounded through the air, stopping the bear in his tracks. We both looked up to see a sphere of fire enveloping both dragons.

Whose fire it was, I couldn't tell. All I could see were the two dragons flying at each other, jaws open, ready to kill.

"Callum..." I moaned, horrified.

I couldn't see how anyone could come away from such a conflict alive.

Snarling, the bear pulled his eyes to me once again and leapt into the air, ready to come down on me with all its might.

I slammed my eyes shut and called out to the first image I could summon into my mind.

A semi-circle of archers, standing between us, their bowstrings tight, arrows at the ready.

When I opened my eyes, as if it was all happening in slow-motion, I saw the apparitions, ghostly, otherworldly, and deadly. Their conjured bodies weren't made of flesh and bone, but flame, licking at the air to form the loose outlines of men.

They were Fire Spirits, conjured to do my bidding.

Callum's words flashed through my mind:

The flame wasn't coming from me...

*It was coming from **you.***

I had taken possession and control of one of the elements. Just as Solara and the other Witches could do. I'd created creatures of flame. Ghostly apparitions, their bodies indestructible and powerful.

The bows in their hands were made of black wood, inlaid with gleaming mother of pearl. The arrows, too, were the deepest black, and at their ends were spikes of shining silver.

As the bear surged through in the air, the bowmen loosed their arrows.

The bear's torso twisted, let out a gruesome wail, then crashed to the ground.

The bowmen disappeared, their weapons falling to the ground and fading to smoke.

But the arrows remained, buried deep in the bear's flesh.

Horrified, I leapt forward, crying out Lachlan's name, tears streaming down my face.

Slowly, the bear's form faded, and all I saw was my friend—the friend I'd known, his eyes back to their vibrant green, his face all charm and innocence—staring up at me.

Five arrows pierced his flesh. His leg, his left shoulder, his right side, his stomach…the right side of his chest.

It was the arrow in his chest that frightened me most.

"Vega," he croaked, a drop of blood at the corner of his mouth.

I choked back a sob to realize that his lung had been punctured.

"Don't…" I said. "Please, don't talk."

He shook his head weakly, even as I blinked my tears away.

"You were right," he murmured.

"Right about what?" I asked.

"That…person. It…wasn't me. It was never me."

DEEP WOUNDS

I KNELT BEHIND LACHLAN, cradling his head in my lap as I pulled my eyes up to the sky once again. There was no longer a sign of either dragon. I couldn't see who'd won, who'd lost...

Or if they'd both lost.

My shoulders hunched, my frame caved in, and I cried, my tears landing in Lachlan's dark curls like a bitter rain shower.

I was still in that position when I heard a gentle voice call my name.

~Vega.

Callum? Is that you? What's happened?

~I'm all right. We have Meligant on the run. You need to get the Seekers and leave. Now. If this goes badly, the silver dragon will come back for you.

But Lachlan is hurt...

~I know. Meligant knows, too...and he's angry enough to burn the whole world to the ground. Do what you can and get away. Please. I love you...

And then, he was gone.

Lachlan was still breathing, though I could hear a horrible, struggling rattle each time he inhaled.

He was in so much pain.

And it was all because of me.

I closed my eyes and reached out with my mind to the one person who could help him. The one person who would do anything in her power to heal him, to bring him back from the dark place he'd been inhabiting for too long.

Solara...

I felt her on the air before I saw her.

"Vega," she said softly. "Rise to your feet. You have a job to do."

Carefully laying Lachlan's head on the ground, I obeyed, pulling myself up and turning to face the Witch.

"Will he be okay?" I asked. "Will he..."

I couldn't finish the question. The possibilities were too cruel.

"He will survive, with the help of Maeve, Luna, and the others," Solara said, her eyes on Lachlan's face. "I won't let him out of my sight, I promise."

"His father," I said. "He'll come for him. If you take him back to Aradia..."

"Let him come. He may have a dragon, but dragons aren't the only ones who can fly."

I choked out a sob then—an almost happy one, to see the fight in her eyes. "Thank you," I said, throwing my arms around her.

She held me for a few seconds before pulling away and saying, "Your Seekers...you need to bring them to the Academy. You need to go—now."

I nodded. "The Orb," I said. "I left it inside. I never took it. I don't know if..."

"Have some faith in your friends," Solara said, laying a soft hand on my shoulder. "They're called Seekers for a reason. Now, go. Leave this place, for their sake. Do not delay."

With a final nod and a weak attempt at a smile, I closed my eyes, and a moment later, opened them to see myself surrounded by Seekers, their chests heaving, their chainmail still intact. We stood in a circle in the eastern courtyard of the Academy.

All were accounted for, and aside from a few scratches, all of them were miraculously unharmed.

"Oh, thank God," I said, looking at Meg first. Sweat drenched her brow, which she wiped with the sleeve of her silver tunic.

"I'm so sorry," I told them. "I had to get Lachlan away from you all. I didn't know what he'd do if he got his hands on the Orb again...I suppose it's gone for good."

"Gone?" Desmond said, a puzzled look on his face. "Why would you say that?"

"Because I left it on the table," I said. "You were all busy fighting. I should have grabbed it."

"Pfft," Desmond said with a laugh.

And then the others started laughing, too. They looked downright giddy, considering our utter failure.

"What?" I asked, annoyed. "What's the joke?"

"It's actually a good one," Desmond said. "It starts with *'The Orb of Kilarin walked into an Academy...'*" He reached under his loose-fitting mail and extracted the glowing purple sphere. "You didn't think I was pregnant, did you?"

My eyes nearly leapt out of my head when I saw the Orb.

"Des! How did you..."

"Sleight of hand, remember? Your granddad taught me. He must've known it'd come in handy someday. It was the only way to steal it from those brainless guards. No sense of humor whatsoever, those wanks."

"To be fair," Meg said, "Olly froze those two brainless guards in place so they couldn't have defended the Orb even if they'd wanted to."

"I'd hug you all, but I'm worried that the Orb would go crashing to the ground," I laughed.

"Well, then," Desmond said, "let's get it to your grandfather, so we can have a proper group hug. Then, let's eat."

EPILOGUE

IT WAS two hours before Callum and Caffall returned to the Academy, and I was in the eastern courtyard with Niala to greet them when they finally arrived.

The gash in Caffall's wing was horrifying to look at, but after examining it for a minute, Niala assured me he would heal.

"Dragons are remarkable creatures," she said. "And our friends at the Aradia Coven have taught me a great deal about balms. I can help him. He'll be good as new in no time."

I thanked her. "Honestly, I'm amazed that's the only injury either of you sustained," I told Callum when I'd hugged and kissed him enough to satisfy me for a few minutes. "When I saw that ball of fire in the sky—what *was* that, anyhow?"

Callum grinned, turning to Caffall, who let out a quiet sort of snort.

"It seems our friend here has some tricks up his sleeve," Callum said.

~I merely trapped the silver dragon in a sphere of flame so that Meligant wouldn't be able to steer him away and harm you, Seeker. Not being able to see, Mardochaios thrashed and struggled against it. I

managed, after some time, to force him to a distant field, where I freed him from the sphere, and he threw his rider from his back.

"Wait—seriously? Meligant fell? Is he…"

"He's not dead," Callum said. "Though he probably won't be walking for some time. And I can't imagine Mardochaios is going to let him on his back anytime soon. The beast flew south, and I'm not sure why he'd ever return."

"One small victory, I guess," I said.

"And Lachlan?" Callum asked. "Is he…"

"I'll visit him when Solara says his wounds have healed enough. I just hope his mind can recover from whatever his father did to him."

"Something tells me he will," Niala said. "He's always been strong. And his heart is good. He may even be a valuable ally in the war to come."

"Speaking of war," Callum said, nodding toward a set of doors at the far end of the courtyard. "Here comes our fearless leader."

"Not always fearless, Lord Drake," Merriwether said as he made his way toward us, the Orb of Kilarin in his hands.

"Another success," he said. "I owe all our Seekers my thanks."

"And we owe you thanks for teaching Desmond whatever trick it was that brought the Orb to you," I replied.

Merriwether pulled the sphere up to eye level and stared into its depths. "Indeed," he said. "It's already begun to serve its purpose."

"What do you mean?"

"I've seen the Usurper Queen. Her movements. Her plans. It is time that I begin preparing for battle."

"Wait—*you*?" I asked. "I thought Callum was in charge of the Academy's troops."

Merriwether lowered the Orb, leaned forward, and said, "Surely you know I'm good for more than just opening doors in the Academy, Vega dear. War is coming…and at long last, the time has come for me to play my part."

.   .   .

End of Book Five, *Seeker's Hunt.*

COMING SOON: SEEKER'S PROPHECY

Summer is coming, and with it, the final battle for the throne of the Otherwhere.

After the recent mayhem, Vega is preparing for the fight of her life. Will Good prevail over Evil, or will the Usurper Queen prove that the Prophecy was wrong all along?

Old friends, new enemies, and those who sit somewhere in between will all be put to the test in this final installment of the Seeker's Series!

ALSO BY K. A. RILEY

If you're enjoying K. A. Riley's books, please consider leaving a review on Amazon or Goodreads to let your fellow book-lovers know!

DYSTOPIAN BOOKS

| RECRUITMENT | RENDER | REBELLION |

THE EMERGENTS TRILOGY

  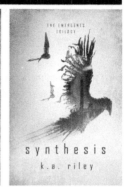

| Survival | Sacrifice | Synthesis |

THE TRANSCENDENT TRILOGY

| Travelers | Transfigured | Terminus |

ACADEMY OF THE APOCALYPSE

Emergents Academy | Cult of the Devoted |

Army of the Unsettled

THE RAVENMASTER CHRONICLES

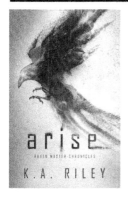

| Arise | Banished | Crusade |

THE CURE CHRONICLES

VIRAL HIGH TRILOGY

Apocalypchix | Lockdown | Final Exam

THE THRALL SERIES

Thrall | Broken | Queen

ATHENA'S LAW

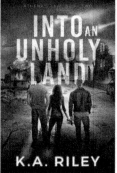

Rise of the Inciters

Into an Unholy Land

No Man's Land

FANTASY BOOKS

FAE OF TÍRIA SERIES

A Kingdom Scarred

A Crown Broken

Printed in Great Britain
by Amazon

43834738R00142